P9-DMR-093
Kissing
Snowflakes

Kissing Snowflakes

ABBY SHER

Point

ISBN-10: 0-545-00010-6
ISBN-13: 978-0-545-00010-9

Text design by Steve Scott
The text type was set in Bulmer.

12 11 10 9 8 7 6 5 4 3 2 7 8 9 10 11 12 /0

Printed in the U.S.A.
First printing, November 2007

For my mom and dad, who told me I could do anything as long as I brushed my hair.

I would also like to say thank you to Aimee, Abby, and Molly for their great insight and inspiration. To Sam A., Sam B., Sara, Gabra, Jo, Megan, Susan Shapiro, Paula Derrow, the Tigers, and Simonie Alice. And to my loving family, especially Mr. Bird.

Kissing Snowflakes

Chapter 1

Beep beep!

"Hey, kid, you want a lift?" Dad pulled up to the curb in a bright blue rental Explorer, and stuck his head out the window like an eager puppy. My brother, Jeremy, was in the back, staring out the opposite window. Kathy was in the passenger seat, a wide smile plastered across her face.

"Sure," I said, throwing my duffel in the trunk. I was the last one out from the baggage carousel because they had thought my bag was missing. That's kind of how I felt today, like a lost, limp bag, on my way to who knows where. I climbed in next to Jeremy.

"The fun starts now, kids!" said Dad. His eyes went back and forth between the two of us in the rearview mirror. They were so wide and hopeful, and I could see how important it was for him that this be true.

"Yippee!" said Kathy, clapping her hands.

Dad wound his way out of the Burlington, Vermont, airport and onto the open road. The mountains rose up around us, great snowy peaks etched against a lilac sky. It was already afternoon. The sun hung low, slowly sifting into fiery reds and oranges, spreading its warm glow over everything. It really was beautiful. Dad navigated us through the roads swiftly and smoothly. He was an excellent driver. So steady and calm. I always felt safe with him at the wheel.

"Ah, isn't that breathtaking?" he sighed, reaching for Kathy's hand out over the console.

"This is gonna be a total blast!" she said, leaning on his arm.

I wanted to tell her that nobody said "total blast" anymore. I think that went out soon after "gag me with a spoon." But I kept my mouth shut and just sighed to myself.

I knew I was being a snot. I knew I should've been enjoying the view, feeling the rush of the clear Vermont air, losing myself in the majestic trees towering above us, draped in their dresses of snow. But I felt miserable, watching Dad and Kathy all snuggly in the front seat. Her shiny dark hair fell over her shoulders and she was oohing and aahing as Dad steered us through patches of trees, winding past sleepy villages with tall church steeples, lopsided wooden fences, and an old-fashioned pharmacy called Canfield Corners.

Dad and Kathy. Kathy and Dad.

How had we come here?

Well, we had just flown in from Florida, where Dad and Kathy got married.

Wait. Back up.

It started that night when Mom and Dad announced they were taking some time to "find themselves." Dad was pacing around the dinner table with his hands in his back pockets. He wouldn't sit still. Mom was pushing her lamb chop back and forth across the plate. Jeremy was chewing his Tater Tots — with his mouth open, of course. He always chewed with his mouth open even though he was two years older than me. Mom usually asked him to please close his mouth while he was eating. Dad did, too. But that night, nobody said anything about it.

"So, Mom and I have been talking and let me start this by saying that this came after some long and hard thought. We have really tried to make this work and we don't know what to do right now except this. And I mean, it doesn't feel right, but really nothing has felt right for a long time. For a long, long time. And so . . . well, we've decided to separate for a while. So, this is just for now. Or for — jeesh, I'm doing a lot of talking. Sarah, do you want to add anything?"

Mom shook her head. Her gray hair swished and then fell back into place and she tucked it behind her ears, but she wouldn't look up from her plate.

"Do you have any questions for us? Jeremy? Samantha?" That's me. Samantha. Samantha Iris Levy. Usually everybody calls me Sam, though. And when I'm talking to myself, I call myself Levy. I know, it's kinda weird. But there you have it.

That was so long ago now. Four years ago, to be exact. Even though it felt like it was yesterday. Even though I could taste it in the back of my throat and feel it pulling my stomach into a tight knot. My hands were sweating and I felt like an overgrown marshmallow in my ski jacket.

It had all happened so fast after that.

Mom stayed in our house (in a little suburb in Westchester, New York), Dad moved about ten minutes away into Chatsworth Towers. His apartment was so small that he made us eggs for dinner and we had to eat them standing up. About a year later, Grandpa got sick, and Dad said he needed to go down to Florida to take care of him. It was supposed to be just for a little while. But the next thing we knew he was moving into his own place down in Orlando, and it had a screened-in porch and a bird feeder where he could see blue jays every morning. Jeremy and I went to visit for a weekend and the whole time Dad had his binoculars out, showing us the difference between the crested flycatcher and the purple martin.

Then he started working at Simmons & Cray as one of the chief financial officers. He said the work was very challenging, an easy commute, and did he mention that he rescued a tree swallow that had fallen out of a branch and that he had started seeing a wonderful woman named Kathy? She was a travel agent, and we would definitely like her because she was a Yankees fan and really into the outdoors and she had a cat named Annette. I tried to tell him that he didn't like cats, but Dad just said, "I thought I didn't. But this is different. Things are different now."

I asked him when he was moving back, and he said

the weather was always sunny, even in October, and then November, and then December.

December 27.

Dad and Kathy set the wedding date so that Jeremy and I could come down for winter break. We flew out on Christmas because Dad found a cheap flight, and besides it's not like we were missing anything, because we're Jewish. Kathy came with Dad to pick us up from the airport in her little red hatchback. Everything about Kathy was petite and perky. She had warm, caramel-colored skin and dark, sparkling eyes above her perfect, tiny nose. When we got out of the car at the condo, she came up to my shoulder.

The wedding was in a little Mexican restaurant in Orlando, because Kathy's family is Mexican. They were married by a justice of the peace, and Dad had this big drooly grin on his face the whole time and then we had really bad Mexican food. The onions in the guacamole gave me a stomachache. The highlight was definitely Grandpa getting up to make a speech at the reception and saying, "You guys are all Mexican, right? So do any of you know what happened to that kid, Elian Gonzalez?"

Kathy's whole family just sat there, stunned. I laughed a little now, in the car, just thinking about it.

"What's that, kiddo?" called Dad over the seat.

"Nothin'," I said.

"I think we're in for a gorgeous sunset," he said.

"I can't wait!" said Kathy, clapping her hands again.

So, that was the story, more or less. And here we were. This was going to be winter break. The four of us were headed to an inn in West Lake, Vermont, for a week of skiing and sitting by the fire, and "getting to know each other." Ugh. I didn't even know how to ski. I had a feeling it wasn't going to come naturally either. I liked running in gym, and I had gone to ballet classes when I was little, but most of the time I was trying not to trip over my own feet. To me, downhill skiing sounded like an invitation to a face dive. Jeremy was psyched, though. He had been skiing a few times with friends and said this time he was going to try snowboarding, too. Dad and Kathy were going to do cross-country, because they heard that was easier to break into. So that left me all alone.

I did have a plan, though. Phoebe and I had talked about it for weeks before. Phoebe was my best friend and we told each other *everything*. She said West Lake was the capital for hot snow studs, and she was sure I was going to find one at the inn. Then I wouldn't have to worry about Kathy or Dad or anybody. I had visions of myself flying down the mountain, my scarf whipping behind me, a tall, dark-haired Adonis holding me firmly by the waist. Or he could be blond. And he didn't have to have muscles. Big muscles kind of ook me out anyway. Just tall. He had to be taller than me. Which meant six feet at least.

Everybody in my family is tall. Dad is 6'2". Jeremy is 6'1". Mom is 5'9" and so am I. It really sucks because most of the guys in my grade are barely my height. Everything about me is kind of long and stringy. My arms, my legs, my hair — which is the color of mud and somewhere between flat and flatter. And I got these long, droopy ears from my dad. That's why I keep my hair long, and I never wear ponytails. It's too embarrassing. Jeremy has the same ears, but he's a boy so he doesn't care. We also both have a bunch of freckles on our faces. The one thing I actually like about myself is my gray eyes. I'm the only one in my family who has them. My mom says they're exotic. But I think she says that mostly because she's my mom. Anyway, I have a thing for eyes. It's the first thing I notice about people.

And I dream about the day when someone will stare all gaga into mine.

It had been so long since I had been with someone. It had been since like — okay, ever. Unless you counted the school play, *The Grapes of Wrath,* where I got to kiss Leo Strumm. He was playing Al, and I was Al's Girl and there was this scene where I said, "I thought you said I was purty," and then he had to kiss me. It was my first real kiss. I mean, I know I'm almost sixteen years old and most people have kissed by then, but I guess I'm a late bloomer and nobody knew it except for Phoebe and my mom but . . . yeah, there it is.

I had practiced long and hard for that kiss. I made Phoebe sit up with me on my bed and we had smothered my pillows with slobbery smooches. It was a good thing that Phoebe was patient. She's definitely more experienced than me. She's just more comfortable around guys than I am. She has red curly hair and cobalt-blue eyes and really pale skin that gets splotches of color whenever she laughs too hard. And she's good at making conversation, cracking jokes, even walking up to complete strangers at parties and introducing herself.

But not me. I don't know what it is. I usually have something to say about *everything*. Seriously. Mom says it's good that I have opinions. And I do make Phoebe and my other friend Rachel laugh. I know how to say *Please take me to your home. I will be a good wife,* in Russian. But around guys I feel like my mouth is full of fuzzy marbles. Sometimes Phoebe has to pinch me in the arm just so I'll say hello. Lately, I've been thinking I should just wear a sign that says *Really, I'm interesting. Give me a chance. P.S. If I pass out, I'm type O-positive.*

Phoebe has kissed a bunch of guys, even dated a few. But a lot of kids in our grade are way ahead of both of us. Like having sex and stuff. Sara Spencer and Kevin Mallon have done it. So have Alissa Paulson and Andy Trotts. And almost everyone on the girls' lacrosse team lost their virginity on the tournament weekend down in Alexandria, Virginia. Meanwhile, I still have Cookie Monster slippers and I like to sleep with my favorite little pillow — but I hope I'll catch up one day soon. At this rate, I'll probably start having sex when I turn forty.

Phoebe said not to give up. That I had to change my attitude. Maybe I was trying too hard. Or not hard enough. I just had to act like myself and act like I *liked* myself and then guys would see that I was fun to be around. And so we had made a pact. This winter break, something was going to happen. We were going to *make* it happen. We were going to wear our shiniest lip gloss and put on our brightest smiles. And we were going to find ourselves some men. Some *real* men.

"Ooh, look at that!" cried Kathy. Two deer leaped across a field after each other, circling playfully around a clump of trees. Hmmrgh. Even deer could find love out here in the woods. There *had* to be someone for me, too, right?

"Did you see that?" Kathy asked, turning around in her seat. Jeremy was asleep, so she looked at me, her eyelashes batting wildly.

"Yeah, we have deer where I grew up, too," I said. I knew it was mean, but I was not in the mood.

Kathy seemed unfazed. "It's just so magical," she sighed, turning around again. "You know what my favorite thing to do is when it's snowing really hard?" she continued.

"What?" asked Dad.

"I love to go outside and spend the afternoon kissing snowflakes."

Dad gave a soft chuckle. "Kissing snowflakes?"

"Yeah! You know, you tilt your head up to the sky and you just let them fall on you. And a lot of them land on your nose or maybe in your eyes and melt. But when you get one, when you really catch the right one on your lips, you *know*."

I could see in the mirror Dad had one of those dumb smiles on his face like at the wedding. Ugh.

"I guess it's kinda silly when I say it out loud," Kathy said, softer now.

"Yup," I mouthed, even though nobody was looking at me.

"No, no! I get it," said Dad. "I think I've spent a lot of time staring up at the sky, waiting, and now I've got my snowflake to kiss." And he leaned over again and planted a big one right on Kathy's perfect rosebud lips.

I thought I was going to break into a million pieces. I was so mad. Why couldn't Dad find that with Mom? I had never seen him call Mom his snowflake, or stare at her all googly-eyed in the car. Most of our road trips had been up to Connecticut to visit Aunt Doris. We played I Spy or listened to Dad's Beatles CDs. Once Jeremy stuck a bean from his bean-bag frog up my nose, and I got a nosebleed trying to get it out. Another time Mom threw up in her pocketbook because Dad was taking the turns too fast. They were never romantic and swoony like this. At least not as far as I could remember.

But more than mad, I was jealous. Jealous that Dad had moved on from us. That he had found love. Or dementia — the jury was still out. And now he started whistling. I hadn't heard him whistle in so long. He was an amazing whistler. It wasn't just plain old songs, either. His whistling dipped and twirled, trilled and slipped in and out of different tunes. Mostly the Beatles. He did it whenever he was really happy. First it was "Help!" and then it slipped into "Paperback Writer," mixed with a little of his favorite, "Let It Be." He had one hand on Kathy's leg, softly keeping time with his music.

"Hey, Dad? Can we pull over? I gotta pee." I didn't really. I just felt like I needed some fresh air. The car felt too small now and all this love stuff was making me a little nauseous.

There wasn't much in the way of gas stations on this road. Mostly just farmhouses and open fields. Dad finally found a place that looked more like a barn with a wooden sign that said FRESH CIDER! in big green painted letters and blue blinking lights in a little window.

The man inside was covered with dirt and sawdust, standing on a stepladder, hammering something into a ceiling rafter. There was a long wooden table covered in glass bottles of syrup, baskets of onions, garlic, and apples, and chalky balls of soap lying out on pieces of wax paper. A cast-iron stove stood in the corner with a pot gurgling on top.

"Sorry, my wife, Dorothy, is getting the last couple of bottles of cider. Should be out in a sec," said the dusty man. I loved the way his rust-colored beard blended in with his brown coveralls.

"No problem," said Dad. "Actually, we were wondering if we could use the restroom."

"Sure, sure," said the man, pointing past the stove to a set of swinging doors that looked like they were from an old-fashioned saloon. I went through and found the bathroom.

When I came out, Dad was standing on a chair, just next to the man.

"You see? It's easy enough. Restructured the whole roof that way," the man was explaining. His voice was warm and crackly.

"Hey, Sam," said Dad. "Norm's just showing me how he put up his own drywall. I've been meaning to do that on the porch in the condo." Norm gave me a smile. His eyebrows were big and bushy, too. When Norm turned back toward the wall, Dad shrugged his shoulders and made a funny face. Dad barely knew how to screw in a lightbulb — I knew he was just listening to Norm to be nice.

I went outside to wait. It was a whole other world here. I looked up. The sky was enormous, hanging on to the last slips of purple, and now I could feel soft flakes falling on my face as I opened my arms and pretended I was floating away with them. Ahhhh. I took a deep breath in and let it out with a deep sigh.

"Sounds like you've got a lot on your mind," came a small voice behind me.

I turned around to see Kathy's bright teeth open in a wide grin.

"I guess," I mumbled.

"You just gotta let it go. Just look up and find a flake and . . . *'smmmwwk'!*" She puckered her lips and squeaked out a kiss.

I stared in horror. Was she for real?

"Come on, try it! It'll make you feel good!" Kathy said, nodding her head fervently.

"Nah, I think I'm okay."

"You sure?" she purred. Now she was standing right in front of me, her head tipped up.

"Yeah, I'm sure."

"Come on, give it a try!"

"Really, that's okay."

Then she reached out one of her pink gloves, like she was going to take my hand. I stuffed mine into my jacket pockets quickly.

"Sam. Is it okay if I call you Sam?" she asked.

"Yeah. That's what everyone else calls me," I said flatly.

"Where does that come from?"

"It's short for Samantha." Were we really having this conversation?

"Yeah, I know. I just thought maybe there was some other . . ." her voice trailed off into the darkening sky. Then it was her turn to let out a sigh. "Oh well," she whispered, and turned away. I headed toward the car. Sorry, Kath. Couldn't she tell that we were *not* buddies? And we were not going to be, either.

I walked around to the far side of the car and slumped down so she couldn't see me. I couldn't believe I had a whole week of this ahead of me. Then I heard the door to the barn open behind me and Dad's voice, low and soft.

"Hey, what're you doing out here, sweetie?"

"Just listening to the sky," she murmured.

"Mmmm, it's something, huh?" he said.

And then she said something too soft for me to get. I decided I was too cold to wait out here anyway. But as I was stepping into the car, there it was. Another "*smmmwwk!*" popping in the air. Dad laughed gently.

"C'mon, you try!" she cooed

"*Smmmwwk!*"

"*Smmmwwk!*"

They drifted, peppering the air with tiny smacking sounds, Kathy giggling the whole time.

Ugh. I was already sick of snowflakes, and we hadn't even unpacked.

Chapter 2

Bishop Inn was a large Tudor house tucked into a copse of fir trees at the bottom of a windy hill. There was a long driveway that led us around to the back, where there were four other SUVs, each with its share of pillows and ski poles visible through the back windows. One of the cars was covered with bumper stickers — SAVE OUR PLANET, KEEP AMERICA GREEN, and my favorite, MY HYBRID CAN BEAT UP YOUR HUMMER. Dad turned around to face me and Jeremy.

"Okay, where are we, kids?"

It was what he always used to say whenever we got somewhere special. I don't know how or when it started, but our job was to say, "Here!"

And then he'd say, "And when do we start having fun?"

And we said, "Now!"

This time, I just sat there. Jeremy was still asleep.

"Kids?" Dad tried again, this time shaking Jeremy's knee. "You wanna show Kathy how we do it?"

"That's okay, Judd," said Kathy, putting a hand on Dad's wrist. Her fingernails were perfect pearly half-moons. "We're already having fun."

The inside of the inn was warm and smelled like cedar wood. The first thing I saw when we walked through the door was a crackling fire in the fireplace and two big maroon armchairs in front of it. The ceiling was at least twenty feet high and there was a staircase twisting up onto a balcony. The walls were cherry-stained wood and over the fireplace there was a string of small white Christmas lights and a sketch of a group of men hunting with dogs, and somewhere there was a clock ticking quietly. It was really soothing and homey. Well, if I really couldn't ski, and I didn't find the boy of my dreams, at least I had a cozy place to snuggle up and read, right?

"You must be Mr. Levy," said a tall man with little wisps of gray hair sprouting out of his head and a long, thin nose. He smiled and his light blue eyes got lost in his soft wrinkles.

"That's me," said Dad, sticking out his hand.

"Phil Bishop. Nice to meet you."

"Thank you. We're very excited to be here. This is my daughter, Samantha, and my son, Jeremy, and my wife, Kathy."

Wife, Kathy. Deep breaths, Levy, deep breaths.

"Great. Well, let me get you settled in and you can put your things down," said Phil. He led us past the fireplace to a small study lined with books. Outside the picture window was a huge mass of mountains, piled on top of one another, spilling down the countryside.

"Wow," breathed Kathy. And for the first time, I had to agree (even though I didn't tell her that). It was pretty spectacular. I mean, we have trees and some hills in Westchester, but this was different.

Phil was used to the view, I guess. He didn't even look up, just went to his desk in the corner. It was covered with folders, loose scraps of paper, and pink receipts. On top of one of the piles was a glass plate with a half of a ham sandwich and some crumbs.

"Excuse the mess. There *is* a method to this madness," he said, sitting down, pushing the piles into different places on the desk. "Levy . . . Levy . . . Levy. Aha! There we are! The Honeymoon Nest!" He looked up at Dad and gave another big smile. Then he looked at me and Jeremy. "And you'll be going to rooms four and five on the other end of the hall."

"Looks like you ski quite a bit," said Dad, walking over to one of the bookcases.

There were framed pictures on practically all of his shelves. Some of them were of the mountains, but most of them were of what looked like a younger Phil and a beautiful woman with long dark hair and wide, almond-shaped eyes. Most of the time they were in ski outfits, the sun bouncing off their goggles. Then there was one of the woman with a squirming baby in her arms, pink and puckered. Then the three of them — their son, I guessed. He was a cute little kid with the same almond eyes and thin nose. They were posed in front of a Christmas tree, on a sled, and, of course, on skis.

"Yeah, it's hard not to," said Phil. Then he took out a map from under his coffee mug and unfolded it for Dad.

"So here we are. This is the range you're looking at here. Now, you said most of you were new skiers, is that right?"

More like *non*-skiers, I wanted to say.

"First time for all of us except for Jeremy. We can't wait," said Dad, squeezing Kathy's hand.

"Well, this guide will tell you all about the different mountains. I have to say, Sugar Peak's probably your best bet if you're only here for a week. It's about ten minutes away and it's got a lot of different trails — downhill, cross-country, snowboarding. And feel free to ask me or my son, Eric, about anything. We usually try to head out to the slopes sometime in the afternoon for a run. And if you don't see us around, you can always just knock."

He pointed to a door with a brass knocker on it, which was behind his desk. I guessed that was where he lived. Then he opened and closed about five desk drawers and fished out three keys, handing one to Dad and the other two to Jeremy.

"Now, as far as here at the inn, tonight we're having board games and a slide show about local artists. I'm afraid that might not be that exciting for you younger folk. We have an older crowd right now. But maybe tomorrow you'll stick around for our Karaoke Night. And happy hour starts in just 45 minutes or so in front of the fire in the front room."

Dad turned to me and Jeremy.

"Sounds like a plan, huh? We'll meet you down here

in maybe an hour? Have some cocktails, get some dinner?" He put his arm around Kathy's waist. She put her head on Dad's shoulder. It fit there so perfectly, like they were two picture puzzle pieces, sliding into place.

"Actually, I don't need that long, do you?" I said. What, were we all putting on ball gowns and mascara? I had promised Phoebe I'd wear lip gloss, but that wasn't going to take an hour. Besides, I was starving — I hadn't eaten since breakfast back in Florida, and I had slept through the salty cereal and sticks trail mix they gave us on the flight.

Dad's face fell. "Well, we kinda thought we could take an hour to . . . freshen up," he said. Kathy was looking at the ground, but I could see she was blushing.

Oh, great. Now I got it. They had *other* plans. Ew! I mean, I know it happens, but did they have to announce it? Should we make sure Phil knew, too? Maybe put out a flyer along with Karaoke Night? I felt my teeth grinding together.

"That sounds great, Dad," said Jeremy, grabbing my arm and our two bags and pulling me down the hall. "We'll see you downstairs in about an hour."

We found our rooms upstairs, and Jeremy pushed me into one of them and slammed the door.

"What is your problem, Sam?" he spat. His eyebrows came together in a sharp point.

"I don't have a problem. What is *your* problem?" I shot back.

"*I* don't have a problem. *You're* the one with the problem."

"Well, maybe my problem is *you.*"

"Maybe *my* problem is *you.*"

I know, real mature, right?

Usually Jeremy and I get along fine. We used to play together a lot when we were little. Then we went through this couple of years when all he would do was wrestle me until I cried, and I would pull on his ears and try to make them longer. About a year after his Bar Mitzvah he started getting these weird patches of hair on his cheeks and he smelled like sweaty armpits all the time and he sort of stopped talking. I mean he said things like, "Hey, what's up?" and "Get out of the bathroom or I'm gonna pee on your bed." But that's about it.

Now I barely see him. We're in the same high school but we have totally different sets of friends. He spends most of his time in his room or playing poker with his friend Alec. Except when he hogs the television to watch wrestling, or messes up the microwave melting cheese. I don't even know if he's planning on going to college when he graduates. He used to talk about running for city councilman. But I think you have to read more than just the sports section to do that. Anyway, sometimes I miss hanging out with Jeremy. Especially since the divorce. Neither home feels really right to me, and he's the only one who could understand what I'm talking about. I kept wanting to talk with him about the whole Kathy thing, but even at the wedding, the most he had said to me was, "Are you finishing your tamales?" and then he picked off all the cheese on mine. I guess I was hoping on this trip to at least have him to hang out with. To be on my side. But it didn't look like that was happening.

"Listen, Sam. You're trying to ruin this for Dad and that is not cool!" Jeremy's nostrils were flaring now. Even his freckles looked mean.

"I am not trying to ruin this for Dad. I'm hungry!"

"Oh, come on. You're not letting them have any time to themselves!"

"Well, if they wanted to stay in their room by themselves the whole time, then why did they invite us along?" I crossed my arms for emphasis.

"Dad just wants us to all get to know each other."

"Sounds to me like they just want to have cuddle time." I knew I sounded babyish, but I couldn't help it.

"Oh, grow up, Sam. You're just mad because you're not Daddy's little girl anymore. And by the way, it's called sex, not cuddle time."

Leave it to Jeremy to be delicate. He just didn't get it, did he? Sex was one thing I did *not* want to talk about with my brother. Ever.

He took the remote off the top of the television set and turned on MTV. There was a video of a girl singer named Faryll Brea who was about fourteen years old. It felt like every week there was some hottie singer who just got out of preschool with a new album. I wondered if she'd lost all of her baby teeth yet. She was singing about how sometimes she felt so alone she thought she was just a shadow. Like she would know what alone was. She was walking in and out of a big pool in the middle of the woods and she wasn't even pretending to sing all the words. Her sequined dress was making me dizzy. I had to get out of there.

I grabbed my bags off the bed and dumped them in the room next door. Then I dug around for my cell phone and marched down the stairs. Phil was standing in front of the fire now, explaining to an older woman with an explosion of gray frizzy hair about the plumbing systems in older houses like this one.

"As long as you're going to take care of this," the woman said with a thick Boston accent. She looked a little like those pictures of Albert Einstein when he had a big idea. I was so busy watching her head bob up and down that I missed the last step and crumpled down on the landing with a thud.

Nice one, Levy. Martha Graham, here I come.

"Everything okay, Samantha?" called Phil.

"Yup, yup!" I said, and picked myself up, gave him a wave, and slipped out the front door.

The air felt good, even though it was freezing. There was a short slate walk and then a front lawn covered in snow, rolling forward into what looked like a line of fir trees. It was too dark now to make out much except for a wide-open sky with a gazillion stars and a hazy scoop of moon.

I opened my phone and pressed Phoebe's number. I missed her so much. Phoebe always knew what I was thinking, sometimes even before I had time to say it. Like when we hung out in her basement, cutting up magazines, and eating grapes and pretzels. Sometimes we just stayed in her room, lying on the mint carpeting and staring up at the ceiling, not needing to say anything at all. I wished she was here right now.

Phoebe and I had been best friends starting in nursery school. There was a big table in our classroom filled with buckets and toys and salt instead of a sandbox. We were playing with it, and Phoebe dared me to eat a cup of salt. I tried to and threw up all over my blue jumper. Then both of us cried for the rest of the morning. We've been inseparable ever since.

Phoebe and I had been through it all together. Getting our periods. First crushes. My parents' divorce. I spend a lot of time at her house after school. And since she was an only child, there was no one like Jeremy hanging around eating cheese or farting or something. I don't know what I'd do without Phoebe. We had plans to always be friends, and if we could we would live on the same block so our kids could be friends, too. Lately we had talked about moving to New York City after college and sharing an apartment. We went to this store we liked called Seventh Scents and picked out which candles and incense we wanted to light in our windows. We would get a place in the West Village or Brooklyn and adopt some babies maybe from Romania or China and then we'd take care of them together and open a pottery studio or a wine shop.

"'lo?" Phoebe always started talking before she pressed the TALK button. Usually, it made me laugh, but today it just made me miss her more.

"Pheebs! It's me!"

"Sam? Are you okay?"

"No!" I moaned.

"What's going on?" I could just picture her, twirling a piece of hair around her pinky, the curl bouncing back into place.

"Everything!" That was the other great thing about Phoebe. She was a great listener. She didn't try to solve anything or convince me that everything would be okay. She just waited for me to get it all out. I had already called her from the bathroom in the Mexican restaurant, Dad and Kathy's, and the closet back at the baggage claim at the airport.

"My dad is inside with Kathy having sex, and Jeremy is picking his nose in front of the TV, and there are no kids here my age! It's all old people!"

I wasn't sure that was exactly true, but I tend to be dramatic.

"What happened to hitting the slopes and finding love in the mountains?"

"It was too late by the time we got here today. And I'm thinking I'm not even gonna go skiing tomorrow. I'm just gonna fall and make a —"

"Hey, Phoebe! Are you coming back in? We're about to play Murder!" I could hear voices in the background, like someone had just opened a door.

"Be there in a sec!" called Phoebe.

"Where are you?" I asked, but I already knew the answer. She was over at Dave Murphy's house. A bunch of us went over there on the weekends all the time. He had a really cool basement with a Ping-Pong table and a flat-screen TV, and his parents kinda pretended they didn't know when we had wine coolers or beer. We all lived really close to each other so we could walk over or carpool. And we weren't big drinkers, anyway. We mostly watched movies or sometimes we would play games. Murder was this game where everyone sat in a circle, and then one person had to guess who the murderer was. I know it sounds kind of childish, but it's actually pretty smart because you get a chance to defend yourself and then people can challenge you. Like I said, we're not the coolest crowd, but it's fun.

I could hear Sara and Rachel, Dave and Ben. It sounded pretty crowded, actually. Maybe Dave's older brother, Mark, had brought friends home from college. Lucky Phoebe. But the one voice I was listening for was, of course, Leo's.

Leo. Leo Strumm. I knew it was just a play, but that kiss was really important to me. A little too important, I guess. Leo hung out at Dave Murphy's sometimes, too. Leo was tall — 6'1¾"! (I asked) — and had deep, dark eyes, almost black. He played drums in a band called Lame Duck, and he chewed on his lip whenever he was lost in thought. And he always carried around a copy of *Brave New World* in his back pocket. Okay, yeah, I know that's a little geeky, but to a nerd like me, that's also kinda sexy. The only thing was, Leo barely talked. At least not to me. And I had tried, believe me. But every time I did, he looked overwhelmed. Once he even said, "Sam, aren't you tired?" after I told him about my views on gun control. I told you I have an opinion on just about everything. Plus, my mom has always made sure Jeremy and I read the newspaper at least three times a week.

"Is it okay if you play next round, Phoebe?" I heard someone asking now.

"Yeah, sure!" said Phoebe.

"I'll save you a seat!"

That voice was easy to recognize. It was Madalena, Rachel's foreign exchange friend from Venice. She gave a whole new meaning to the word "sexy." She was gorgeous, with long, wavy brown hair and these eyes that were every color of green mixed together. She wore European jeans and turtleneck sweaters that clung to her every curve. And she was curvy. There must be something in Italian water or something because sixteen is way different over there. Madalena was really sweet, too. Which sucked, because I couldn't hate her. Even that one night . . .

It was at the cast party after *Grapes*. We were all at Dave's, of course. And I was hoping to talk to Leo alone maybe. I didn't know what I was going to say, but we had just shared saliva, so I had to make my move, right? Phoebe and I had rehearsed a couple of options, my favorite one being, "Hey, I think I left my dentures in your mouth. You mind if I look for them?" But I never had a chance to even get through "Hey." As soon as we got to Dave's, I watched Leo slink into a corner with

Madalena where they stayed all night sipping wine coolers and talking into each other's necks. I guess he did know how to string a sentence together after all. I was crushed. She wasn't even in the play! How could he be so shallow as to fall for some smart, sophisticated, disturbingly beautiful young *woman*? Especially when I was offering him a lifetime of awkward conversations and inexperienced lips. And if he was nice to me, a game of Boggle. (Everybody's got to be good at something.)

Ugh. That was not a pretty night. I had even put on a tight miniskirt and one of Phoebe's baby tees, which I kept on tugging at to make sure my belly button didn't show. I got kind of drunk on some red punch that tasted like cough syrup, and I announced to everyone that I was going to get an ear job so that someone would find me attractive. Then for the grand finale I threw up in Dave's driveway. Good times, right?

After that, there was that month or so when Alan Neumar kept on waiting by my locker and asking if he could see my Chemistry homework. Alan was in the play, too — he was a migrant. Alan had saggy eyes like a basset hound's, and I heard he couldn't shower in the boys' locker room because he had a contagious foot fungus. I don't mean to be superficial, but those things aren't exactly turn-ons. And he didn't really talk either, except to tell me I had nice handwriting, but I had misspelled "alkaline." Great.

"Sam? Are you there?" came Phoebe's voice.

"Oh, yeah. Sorry. What'd you say?"

"I said, what if you tried it out? I bet there'd be kids our age there."

"Tried out what?"

"Skiing, dorko."

"Yeah, I dunno. I'll see how I feel. What else have *you* guys been doing?"

"You know. We ordered pizza, and some people were watching a movie that Mark and his friends made at school. It's pretty funny. About frogs. And then some people went over to Bonnie Briar to go sledding. The rest of us are playing Murder. The usual."

"That sounds awesome right now." I sighed.

"Oh, come on, Sam. So, tell me about the inn. Is it pretty?" I knew she was working hard to cheer me up, so I tried to sound chipper.

"Yeah, I guess."

"You sharing a room with Jeremy?"

"Ew, no way."

"Well, that's good. What else?"

"Nothing. Tonight they're having a slide show. Woo-hoo."

"Well, why not curl up in front of the fire? Just relax. And then tomorrow you can hit the slopes and find some fun people to hang with. Remember — you're on a mission," she said.

"Yeah, I know, it's just I —"

"Pheeb! Come on! We need you in here!"

"Next round. Promise," said Phoebe.

"It's okay, Pheebs. You can go," I said, even though I wanted so badly for her to stay.

"No, that's all right. Tell me more about the mountains."

"Well . . . they're tall. And snowy. I don't know. Tell me about Mark's friends."

"Oh! There's this one guy, Paul, who's super dreamy. I think he might be Greek originally, but he lives in New York now. He's studying philosophy and he has this big space in between his front teeth. And then there's Mark's roommate, Beezus."

"Beezus?"

"Yeah, I think because there's a Scott R. and a Scott B., and he's Scott B. But anyway, he is really funny and he's staying with Mark because he's from Montana and it's too expensive to go home. He's like nineteen I think because he took off a year before school to fix houses for people in Nepal. I think he's going back there this summer, too. How cool is that? I was trying to get on the Internet so I could look up Nepal's biggest export or something. How's this sound, 'Hey, so I heard there's really good paprika over there. I *love* paprika, don't you? It's so spicy.'"

Phoebe always knew how to cheer me up. She was laughing, too.

"Oh, Pheebs. I wish you were here. Then it'd be fun."

"Yeah, well, you're just gonna have to have fun for both of us."

"Yeah, I guess. First I have to deal with Ricecake." Ricecake was our nickname for Kathy, because ricecakes are so bland and they're made of mostly air.

"Ah, just ignore her. This is your time to have fun."

"Yeah, you're right. I know."

"Phoebe?"

I didn't recognize the voice on the other end now. Must've been one of Mark's friends.

"Yeah?" Phoebe sang sweetly.

"Who is it? Who is it?" I asked.

"Paprika," she whispered.

I felt a flutter in my chest. That was the best part of our friendship. I always got to live a little vicariously.

"Hey, a bunch of us are going to head out to Bonnie Briar, if you wanted to come with?" I couldn't tell. Did he have a Montana accent? Was there such a thing?

"Oh, I guess I'll meet you in a little bit," said Phoebe.

"GO! GO!" I barked.

"Are you sure?" I could tell Phoebe was putting her face really close to the phone. Her voice was so close my ear felt itchy.

"Yes! Yes! But Pheebs?"

"Yeah?"

"I don't think it's paprika. It's probably something like wool or lentils."

"Got it," she said.

"And call me later. I want a full report."

"Definitismally."

I shut my phone. If Pheebs fell in love and moved to Nepal, I was going with her, even if I had to pitch a tent in her backyard. I'd be the spinster who wove blankets and cooked stews. Maybe I'd get a sheep of my own, too. At least then I wouldn't be completely alone.

I pressed my mom's number. I hadn't spoken to her since Jeremy and I left for Florida, even though I wanted to call her so badly while I was hiding during the wedding reception. But I knew that would be hard for her, so I didn't.

Four rings and then it went to voice mail. I clicked my phone off. Where was she on a Sunday night? She usually stayed home and read the paper. Unless Lois invited her over for a glass of white wine. Or maybe she went out with Jon.

Ugh, Jon. Talk about a nerd. Jon had picked up Mom at the nursing home where she worked. I think he came in to play clarinet or something. He was good at the clarinet because he had this long, droopy lower lip. He was also 6'2", which was something, I guess. And he liked to take Mom to concerts at Lincoln Center and out for Chinese food. But he also talked way too close to my face, he had a thin, gray ponytail, and he was constantly chewing on mint toothpicks. Definitely not cool enough to be dating my mom. My mom is fun and smart and has the softest hair in the world and she can do the *New York Times* Sunday crossword *in pen* in less than two hours. And when we were little she used to take us on roller coasters at Rye Playland, even though it made her so scared that she had to put her head between her knees afterward. She also used to make batik shirts for us with stars and spaceships on them. She really is awesome. What was my dad's problem? I knew it was more complicated than that, but still, I wouldn't be out here in the middle of Nowheresville right now if he could see how great Mom was, right?

I saw a warm shaft of light open and spread out on the snow as the front door to the inn opened.

"Sam, is that you?"

Exactly *not* what I needed right now.

"Yeah. Hi, Kathy," I said limply.

"Phew! We've been looking all over for you. We were going to have some drinks and then sit down to dinner. What do you say, Miss Supercool?"

Miss Supercool? What were we, like, five years old?

I looked up. Kathy had changed into a long cowl-neck sweater and skinny jeans. Her hair was pulled back, too, and piled on top of her head. Of course, she had perfect, delicate, tiny ears.

"Listen, Kathy. Just go ahead without me. I don't really feel that hungry after all." I tried to give her a fake smile and then looked back at the ground.

"You okay?" she asked.

"Yeah, sure."

I didn't look up. Eye contact could be construed as an invitation to talk more. But I guess she couldn't take the hint because she came and sat next to me on the stone step anyway.

"It's cold out here. You should have a coat on."

"I'm fine." Why couldn't she see that I just wanted to be alone?

"Listen, I'm sorry this is so hard for you, Sam. I really am." I felt her hand touch my back tentatively, like spider fingers. "I mean, here I am, suddenly in your life. I'm nothing like your mom, you know? I'm this totally new, different bird."

What was *that* supposed to mean?

"And I know you have a very special relationship with your father. I really respect that, and I see how much you love him. And I love your father very much, too. Which must be hard. I get it. I really do." Now she was sort of massaging the back of my neck, but it was really light and just next to the tag so mostly it just felt scratchy and annoying. I knew she was trying, but I couldn't help it. I had had enough.

"Do you get it? Do you really?" I said. "Because I

don't see how you could! Honestly, Kathy, no offense, but none of this would be happening if it wasn't for you."

Her eyes got big and she was blinking a lot.

"Well, I'm sorry you feel that way, Sam, I'm just trying to —"

"No, I know you're trying. Everybody's trying. We're *trying* to work this out, and then we're *trying* to make this easy on you, and then we're *trying* Florida, and try, try, *try*. But I don't want to *try* anymore!"

I could feel the back of my neck getting hot. My nose was drippy and I saw spit flying out of my mouth in the light from the inn. Like I said, I'm no stranger to speaking my mind. Even if it's not pretty.

Kathy took a controlled breath and nodded her head slowly. "Well, okay, then. I just came out to tell you the whole family is sitting in front of the fire and —"

But I wasn't done. As a matter of fact, I was just getting started.

"No, don't you get it?! We are *not* a family! I am *not* your daughter, and you can't tell me when to eat dinner or when to put on a coat!"

"I wasn't trying to tell you what to do," she whined.

"I just wanted you to . . ." She left the sentence in mid-air and shook her head.

"What? Wanted to what?" I pushed.

"I don't know," she mumbled. I knew I should stop, but it made me mad that she wouldn't even stick up for herself.

"You know what, Kathy? I know you make my dad happy and that's great and maybe Jeremy can sit there and act like it's all good and fine, but I can't! You are *not* my mom, and you are *not* my friend, and you are not going to be, okay?! I do not want to watch sunsets with you or see you snuggle with my dad and I certainly will not be kissing any snowflakes. Ever!"

Told you I could be dramatic. I was standing up now, my hands on my hips. And even though I knew I was being a big brat, I have to say, it felt good. I wasn't just screaming at Kathy now. I was letting it out at Dad and at Jeremy and at Leo and a little at Mom and a lot at Jon and his ponytail and his horrible lower lip.

Kathy looked at her hands in her lap, wiggling her pink fingernails. She looked like a little girl who had just gotten punished.

"If that's the way you feel," she said, standing up awkwardly. She still wouldn't look at me, but I could see the corners of her eyes were damp. I had never been this nasty to anyone before.

"It is," I said as firmly as I could.

"But I just want to say, for what it's worth, that this is weird for me, too," she said, still talking to her shoes. "I mean, it took me thirty-eight years to find the person I wanted to be with, and all of a sudden I have two teenage kids, too, and it's great and it's wonderful, but it's a lot to adjust to all at once, and I know you don't need to know this, but I just thought I'd say it so you . . . so you knew, I guess."

Her words spilled out so fast, it looked like her mouth was moving without her controlling it. And then she looked up at me and mashed her lips into this painful half smile. Her cheeks were dark and wet now. This time I was the one who had to look away. Then all I heard was her boots squeaking as she walked back into the inn.

Nice, Levy. Real nice. I sat back down on the slate steps and tried to calm my breath down, pulling my fleece in tighter and wiping my nose with my sleeve.

"Wow. I guess you told her," said a raspy voice.

I looked up. It was a guy, tall and lanky. I guessed he was probably Jeremy's age. Long, thin nose. I couldn't tell what color his eyes were in this light. He was looming over me, blocking out the moon. He had on a big, thick sweater and a scarf tucked around his neck. His dark hair hung down just above his eyes.

"She must've pissed you off, huh?" he asked.

"Excuse me?"

"I mean, you were really letting her have it."

Great. Had he watched that whole thing?

"Well, she was . . ." I started. My voice sounded unsteady. "Did you see . . . ?"

"Yeah." He cut me off. "Pretty harsh," he added. Then he just stood there, waiting for me to respond.

"Well, I mean, I didn't know you were there. Do you always sneak up on people like that?" I knew it sounded snooty, but I was feeling pretty defensive now. Who *was* this guy, anyway?

"No. Not always," he said. "Do you always make grown women cry?"

Whoa. That one landed right on my chest. I felt the cold stinging my skin. For once in my life, I didn't have anything to say.

"Listen, whatever," he said. "I know moms can be a pain sometimes."

I know I should've just let it go. But of course, good old Levy . . .

"That's the thing. She's not my mom. She's my dad's new — Kathy."

"Uh-huh."

This guy was infuriating!

"She's not my mom. She's nothing like my mom. In fact, she probably comes up to my mom's navel. But you know what? It's none of your business, anyway. You don't know who she is or who I am or anything!"

"You're right," he said calmly.

All right, Levy. Just walk away. It's not worth it. But the more this guy stood there with his arms crossed, just looking out into the nothingness, the madder I got.

"You know, I didn't want to come here. I don't even plan on skiing. This whole trip is a big waste of time, and now I have to get a lecture on how to respect my elders?! You can think whatever you want. I really don't care. You can stay out here and spy on people all night, if that's your thing. But I'm freezing and hungry and tired and . . . done!"

I tried to make a sweeping exit by spinning on my heels and stomping back into the inn. But one of my feet had fallen asleep, so it was more like a dramatic hobble. It felt pretty lame. Then I pulled open the heavy wooden door to the inn and let it slam behind me. At least it was warm in here. People were gathered in small groups, chatting and sipping drinks. I really was famished, but I didn't see how I could join the family for dinner now. Dad and Kathy were sitting by the fire playing cards. They didn't even look up when I came in the room. Neither did Jeremy, who was leaning on the mantel with some girl in a fuzzy cream-colored sweater laughing next to him. I wanted to tell her that he ate with his mouth open and that he never flossed. But I didn't.

Instead, I took two red delicious apples from the basket on one of the side tables and went up to my room. Someone had come in and turned the covers down. I was too cold to get undressed, though. I turned on the bathroom sink to run my hands under the hot water. It sputtered and spit out some brown-colored water. Great. But then it ran clear and the steam started rising from the sink. I put my hands under until they turned red, then quickly stripped down and slipped into my sweatpants, a thermal, and my warmest socks.

I slid into the bed, turned on the television, and flipped around. There was some reality show on where the contestants were all trying to put together a puzzle. The puzzle was made of big wooden pieces, and it was supposed to turn into a map that would show them the way to a box of fruit on this island. Or something like that. I always thought that I'd be good on one of those shows. I love puzzles, and I'm really good under pressure. But I also get lost a lot, especially when I'm walking or on a bus or something and I zone out. And I guess tonight I had proven I wasn't much of a team player. All right, maybe I wouldn't be good on one of those shows.

I rubbed my apple on my shirt and took a bite. I could just picture Jeremy ordering a big steak and chewing with his tongue hanging out. Dad would go for the pasta — and Kathy? Probably a side salad or something skimpy like that. Ugh. What did it matter now, anyway? I took another bite of my apple and wiggled down under the covers until all that was left above the sheets was my head.

I knew I was acting like a baby. I knew I was being unfair to Kathy. I was just so mad at her for taking my dad away. I felt so lonely. It was like everyone had someone special in the world except for me. Even Jeremy with his new fuzzy girlfriend. Even the people running across the TV screen, holding hands as they searched for clues.

I put my apple core on the night table and turned out the light. For a minute, I thought there was something wrong with the switch. It was still so bright in the room. The moon poured in through the window, making the ivy leaves on the wallpaper look mystical as they climbed up to the ceiling. I had to admit, it really was pretty amazing. Even through those four little panes of glass, the sky was so immense and vast and long in every direction. Much bigger than at home. A gazillion stars blinking and spreading out into the night. All I wanted was to be able to share that sky with someone. That was my wish. Just to have someone look up and point out Orion or trace the Big Dipper.

Was it too much to ask?

And then I did something I hadn't done in a long time. I knew it was corny, but I tipped my head back and whispered it up at the moon. I didn't know whom I was asking or how it could be answered, but I did it anyway.

Please let me find someone to share this sky with. Please?

And then I closed my eyes, and I waited to see what would happen.

Chapter 3

When I woke up, it was still a soft bluish pink in the room. I looked at the clock.

5:48.

I guess that's what happens when you go to sleep before ten o'clock.

I tried closing my eyes again but it was pointless. I was wide awake. And starving. *All right, Levy. Have to make the best of this situation. Start over. Try to be civil to Kathy. Or maybe just ignore her. But first, food.*

I crept into the bathroom and splashed some cold water on my face, then dug through my duffel to find my favorite hoodie sweatshirt and grab my copy of *The Catcher in the Rye*. It was my favorite book. I had read it about twenty times, but I had finished the other book I bought in Florida and all I had from the airport were trashy magazines about women eating their way to being younger and celebrity couples splitting up. I crept downstairs.

There was already a fire going in the fireplace in the lobby, and there was classical music playing, but I couldn't tell where it was coming from. I wandered through to what I guessed was the dining room. There were about a dozen tables set, and floor-to-ceiling windows on one side of the room. The sun was coming up over the snow-covered peaks, turning everything the most incredible color. It was somewhere between orange and pink and purple and it made the snow gleam.

Phil came out of a swinging door on the other side.

"Whoa! We've got an early riser! What can I do for you?"

There were bags under his eyes and the gristle of a new beard growing in, but he still gave a huge smile. His teeth were long and thin, just like the rest of him.

"Oh, I'm fine. I just couldn't sleep," I said.

"Well, let me set you up with a cup of coffee, huh? Breakfast will be coming up soon."

I could hear Mom saying, "Don't drink coffee. It'll stunt your growth."

But I loved the taste of it with just a little whole milk and sugar. Mmm. I was on vacation, right?

"Sure," I said. "Is it okay to sit here?"

"Sure. Or go sit in front of the fire. I love doing that in the morning," said Phil, and then he disappeared back through the door. I could hear plates clattering together and the sizzling of a grill. It smelled so good. There was definitely something sweet like muffins baking and maybe even bacon frying. I was so hungry I wanted to eat my shirt.

I went back to the fire and sat down in one of the maroon armchairs. There was a pile of outdoor magazines on the coffee table and a handmade flyer that said KARAOKE MONDAY! 8:30 IN THE LIVING ROOM! SING TO THE STARS! The last time I had done karaoke was in a booth at my cousin's Bar Mitzvah. I thought I was awesome at the time, singing Madonna's "Like a Prayer." Really getting into it, too — belting it out and even dancing. At the end of the night the DJ gave me a tape of myself that said "Daniel's Rockin' Bar Mitzvah." When I got the tape home and listened to it, I was so embarrassed that I swore I would never do it again. I guess that meant another early night for me. Levy the party animal.

I picked up one of the magazines and opened to "Thirty Hidden Treasures of Vermont." Tried to dive into the pictures of mountains, lakes, and winding trails.

"Are you the one who wanted —" I recognized the voice before I even looked up. It was the guy from outside last night. He held a steaming mug of coffee in his hand, and his mouth was open like he was going to say something else, but he didn't. He drew his eyebrows together above that long nose and almond-shaped eyes . . . and now I knew why he looked oddly familiar. He was the boy from those pictures in the study. Phil's son — Ethan? Evan? He cleared his throat but still didn't say anything. Then he leaned over and put the mug down on the coffee table.

"Thanks," I said.

"Yeah, sure. Listen, I probably should've introduced myself last night. I'm Eric. I live here with my dad."

"Yeah, I know," I said dully.

But he still just stood there.

"And you are . . . ?" he asked.

"Oh, Sam."

"Hi, Sam. Are you reading that?" he asked, pointing to *The Catcher in the Rye* on the coffee table.

"Read it."

"Oh, I love J. D. Salinger. Especially *Franny and Zooey*. Have you read that one, too?"

"Nope."

Then I picked up my coffee cup and blew at the puffs of steam, mostly so I would have something to do. Eric took the hint and walked away. *So much for starting over, Levy*. I guess I've never been good about letting go of grudges. Maybe because I'm a Scorpio. My mom said the first time she fed me liverwurst I got so mad I didn't talk to her for two days. I like to think of myself as principled.

I stirred my coffee. It was milky and sweet, just the way I liked it. And now I heard the swinging door open again, and I could see an older woman in the dining room, carrying a basket that looked like muffins and bagels, then a platter of steaming eggs and one of bacon. My mouth was salivating. It was like that experiment Mr. Keane told us about in Science class, with those dogs and the bell.

As soon as the lady was gone, I made a beeline for the food. Had to close my mouth so I wouldn't drool all over the table while I piled up my plate with eggs and bacon, a warm carrot muffin with butter, and fresh, juicy cantaloupe. Then I plopped back down in front of the fire and started feasting.

Pretty soon an older couple came down the stairs in matching navy fleece sweatshirts. She had a white fluffy helmet of hair and two circles of rouge on her cheeks. He was bald and had tucked his fleece into his tan corduroys. So cute. I watched them go into the dining room. Another couple came down. They were younger and looked like they were Asian or maybe Hawaiian, both with beautiful black, silky hair. Hers was tied in a ponytail that trailed down her back. *Sigh.* I wished I could wear a ponytail. Then a little girl came down, leading what must have been her mom, who was still sleepy-eyed and walking kind of lopsided. Still no single males. Nobody even close to my age. So much for Phoebe's research on West Lake.

A little while later, I heard Dad's voice in the hall. I looked down at my empty plate, then quickly buried my head back in the magazine. I hadn't really figured out what I was going to say yet about last night. I guess I should have rehearsed.

"And then we could see what Mount Seneca is like, if we have the energy for it," Dad was saying. He stopped in front of my chair. "Sam!"

He and Kathy were standing over me now, hands intertwined. Dad was looking straight at me, but Kathy stared at the fire.

"How'd you sleep?" asked Dad.

"Good, good. You?"

"Like a rock."

Silence. *Come on, Levy. Say something nice.* But I wasn't exactly ready to give Kathy a big hug and tell her how happy I was that she was my new stepmom. And she still hadn't even looked at me yet.

Finally, Dad cleared his throat. "Well, something smells good. You gonna join us this morning?" he asked.

"Already ate," I said.

"Okeydoke."

I picked up the magazine again. I didn't want to see Dad's face. I could already tell from his voice how disappointed he was.

An hour later I was towel-drying my hair when there was a knock on the door to my room.

"So, we were going to head over to Sugar Peak today," said Dad, peeking in. "They have downhill, cross-country, and apparently some great instructors."

"Yeah, I think I'm just gonna hang out here," I said.

"Really?"

"Yeah, I'm really into my book right now." *I could read* Catcher *again I guess.*

Jeremy came into the doorway. "So, she's staying here?" he scoffed. "Told you. What are you gonna do, Sam, play solitaire all day?"

"No," I sneered back. Sometimes Jeremy could be such a royal jerk. But he did have a point. I had already tried calling Phoebe after breakfast. No answer. I think today was the day she and her parents were going up to visit her grandma. And I didn't know how many more secret treasures of Vermont I could discover in those stupid magazines.

"Loser," said Jeremy.

"Leave me alone," I grumbled.

"Well, maybe Phil or his son will be around," offered Dad with a shrug. "He told me at breakfast that they were leading a hike for anyone who stayed behind."

Ugh. Not exactly what I had in mind.

"Come on, Dad. I wanna get going before the lines get too long," said Jeremy, walking away.

"Okay, well, see you later . . . ?" started Dad.

His face looked long and droopy.

Levy, don't be a total ass.

"All right," I said. "I'll go."

As it turned out, lots of people had heard about Sugar Peak. The parking lot was full of ski racks and bumper stickers. There were people in line for the lift that took them up to the top, and bright jackets were already zigzagging down in all different directions. They looked so graceful and sure of themselves.

Dad led the way to a little chalet that had a snack bar, wooden picnic tables, a huge Christmas tree and, of course, another crackling fire in the middle with couches around it. It smelled like pine needles and hot chocolate.

There was a big mess of people in the far corner, waiting to get rental equipment. We got in line. Everybody seemed to have on a sporty outfit with long dangling pom-poms and furry hoods. Lots of matching ski pants and striped leg warmers. I looked down at my navy jacket, which my mom and I had gotten on the clearance rack at the end of the season last year, and the red-and-blue-striped mittens that Phoebe and I had picked out together. My scarf was purple, my favorite color, and I had a green hat that looked like a turtle's back and had earflaps. I was also wearing my favorite Levi's with long johns underneath. *Look out Kate Moss, there's a new girl in town.*

"Yeah, I heard it's really icy right now. Superslick,"

one of the guys in front of us was saying. He was shaped like a big rectangle with huge shoulders and a tiny head on top.

"Yeah, we were going down the Falcon Trail at, like, thirty-five miles an hour yesterday!" said the other. He was more of a pear shape, with huge legs. "That's when Seth bit it hard," he added. The two of them laughed a little. Then the third guy spoke up. He was definitely about half their size, and sounded a little worried about the whole thing.

"I feel kinda bad leaving him back there," he said.

"Nah, it's a hospital!" said Rectangle. "There are plenty of nurses and stuff to check up on him. Besides, you heard him. He's gonna be in traction for at least a month. We can visit anytime."

"Yay, Brad. You gotta feel this ice, man, it's incredible!" said Pear.

"All right, all right. This one's for Seth."

"Yay, Seth!" they cheered and then high-fived each other.

That was enough for me. I turned to Dad. "That's where I'll be," I said, pointing to one of the couches by the fire, and then I walked away.

I didn't know mornings could last that long. I drank three and a half cups of cocoa, bit off all my fingernails, and went to the bathroom five times. But mostly, I met Margie. Margie had decided to stay in the chalet that morning, too, just to "let her butt take a break," as she explained. She was from Albuquerque. She lived there with her husband, Stan, and their two ferrets, Elvis and Priscilla. Margie and Stan were retired but they kept very active in the community with their neighborhood watch group, their public transit committee, and their mah-jong league. Margie had a sweater with felt teddy bears that were gathered around a Christmas tree, and she insisted that I try pulling them off and moving them around. (They were attached with Velcro.) She showed me pictures of the ferrets dressed up for Halloween, and the tree house that Stan had built for the grandkids. She really was a sweet lady. But by 10:30 I was seriously considering breaking into sign language to see if she took the hint.

Finally, people started coming in for lunch, their faces flushed, their jackets dusted with snow, their eyes big and bright with excitement.

"Well, I guess I should go try to find my brother and

stuff," I said, standing up and stretching. Margie stood, too.

"You sure you don't want to join us? I know Stan would love to meet you," she said.

"Yeah, my family said we'd meet up, you know . . ." I lied.

"Of course. Well, see you after lunch then, huh?" She smiled and looked at me eagerly.

"Yeah, maybe . . ." I said, backing away into the crowd forming around the grill now.

"Hey, loser," said Jeremy, poking me in the back with his cafeteria tray. "These slopes are amazing! You totally missed out."

"Yo Jer — I'm gonna find us a table near the back, 'kay?" I heard someone say behind us. I turned around. There was a really tall guy, maybe 6'3", with a nest of crazy brown curls and hazel eyes. His shoulders kind of sloped forward, like he was afraid of hitting his head on the ceiling.

"Sure," said Jeremy. "Meet you there."

"Who is that?" I asked, trying to sound casual.

"Oh, that's Aaron. We met on the slopes. He's an awesome skier."

"He's really tall, isn't he?" I asked.

"I guess so," said Jeremy, uninterested.

"Is he over 6'2"? He must be, right?" I asked. But Jeremy was already paying for his cheeseburger and fries.

It was really crowded in the lodge by now. The floor was a big puddle, and it smelled like fried food and sweat. I followed Jeremy to the back where Aaron was sitting at a table that was already full of people who looked like they were our age — three girls and another guy. I spotted Kathy and Dad at a table with two other couples. Dad waved and I gave a small wave back. I hoped he wasn't expecting me to sit with them.

"Jer. Over here," said Aaron.

"Thanks," said Jeremy, sitting down across from him. I squeezed in next to the three girls, who were obviously there together. Two of them had long, silky blond hair, and the third one had a short brown pixie cut. They all had matching sparkles on their eyelids, and they each had cups of yogurt or fruit on their cafeteria trays. Ugh. I really don't like it when girls try to eat "light" all the time. I had ordered a chicken cutlet and fries.

"Hi, I'm Liz," said the one closest to me.

"Sam," I said.

"Heidi," said another.

"Dina!" piped the third.

"We're here on winter break together," explained Liz.

"Cool."

"And Drew's our teacher!" said Dina with a wide smile. Heidi covered her mouth, but I could tell she was giggling.

"That's me," said the guy on the other side of Liz. He had smooth, tanned skin, and eyes that flashed a brilliant blue. There were orange ski goggles on his head and little spikes of dirty blond hair underneath them. He was wearing a gray thermal shirt, but I could tell just from the way it hugged his broad shoulders he was one of those guys who could be an underwear model. Or at least sell fancy watches.

"Yeah, Drew's a really awesome teacher. We learned so much," gushed Liz.

"And he's been in the Olympics!" said Dina.

"Just the trials," said Drew. But I could tell he was pretty pleased they'd brought it up. When he smiled his teeth were bright and perfectly straight. It was a little ridiculous. He looked like a Ken doll. I felt bad, watching the girls all swoon over him.

"That's so amazing. What was that like?" asked Liz.

"Pretty nerve-wracking. I trained for a really long time."

"Downhill?" asked Jeremy.

"Super G," said Drew.

"Wow!" said Dina and Heidi at the same time.

Super G? What the hell was a Super G?

"Yeah, it was incredible," said Drew. "Do you guys ski?" he asked Jeremy and Aaron.

"We hit Eagle's Landing this morning," said Jeremy.

"Yeah, it was awesome," said Aaron. His mop of curls bounced when he talked.

Okay Levy. Come on. Show up.

"Yeah, I heard that's a really cool trail," I said, trying to catch Aaron's eye.

Nothing. I waited.

"Was it fun?" I asked weakly.

"Yeah, I just said it was," said Jeremy. I tried to shoot him a look but he didn't see.

Aaron kept shoving his grilled cheese sandwich into his mouth.

Okay, I could do this. I just needed confidence, perseverance, maybe a blowhorn.

"Sam?" Jeremy was elbowing me in the side.

"Huh?"

"Liz just asked you something."

"Wha — ?"

"Oh, I just said, do you ski, Sam?" asked Liz sweetly.

"Um, not really."

"Really? Why not?"

"Yeah, why not Sam?" asked Jeremy with a sneaky smile.

Great. *Think fast, Levy*. "Oh, you know. I didn't sign up in time. I'll probably take a class tomorrow," I said, giving Jeremy a swift kick under the table.

"Ow!" said Dina, who was sitting across from me.

"Oops! Sorry about that, I didn't mean it! I thought it was . . ." Jeremy watched the whole thing and just shook his head, laughing. Heidi was laughing, too.

"What? I missed it," said Aaron. Ugh.

"Well, if you want, I've got a space or two left in my afternoon session," said Drew.

"You should do it, Sam! It's for total beginners. We had so much fun, we're doing it again!" said Liz.

Jeremy looked at me. "Actually, Sam's more into reading. She's not that into —"

"Yeah, sign me up," I said, cutting him off just in time.

Outside, the air felt thin and sharp. Drew led the group to a small valley just beyond the chalet. Then he stood in front of us with his feet spread apart, and started reading out our names. There was me, Liz, Heidi, Dina, and a little girl named Molly who had pink everything, including earmuffs and knee pads, which I thought was cool. She was there with her dad. And then there was a couple with matching striped hats, I didn't catch their names. I was too busy trying to keep my balance. My boots were a size ten. The guy behind the counter had said that they ran big, but I think he only said that so I didn't feel like a mutant. I knew I would tip over with the first gust of wind.

Drew gathered us in a semicircle.

"Okay, crew. You ready to tackle that mountain? The first thing we're going to do is put on our skis and learn how to stop."

He went around to each of us and made sure that our boots slid into the skis properly. Then he stood in front again and pointed his skis together so they were perpendicular to each other. "This is called the T-stop. It's pretty basic, but it works every time. Can everybody make this shape with their legs?"

Uh, not exactly.

For the next hour and a half, we went over how to stop, how to steer, acceleration and braking, getting on and off the chairlift, and the names of the different slopes. Liz was nodding her head thoughtfully, and Molly kept on bending her knees and practicing her T-stops. I knew I should've been listening. I'm sure what he was saying was important, but I just kept thinking about plowing into a tree and being buried under a pile of snow and wasn't there some news story recently about a guy who had been caught in an avalanche?

"Remember, *you* are in charge here, not the mountain. The most powerful tool you have here is your focus. Maintain your weight on the balls of your feet and keep your knees bent. And leave your behind *behind*." Drew bent his knees and leaned forward, his back making a perfect curve against the white mountain behind him. Out of the corner of my eye, I saw Heidi grab Dina's hand. Drew really *was* extremely good-looking. But it was obvious that he knew it, too, which was a definite turnoff. And behind *behind*? Who thought of that one? I wondered if all the instructors had to say that or if Drew came up with it by himself. It was super cheeseball, if you asked me.

"Okay, now we're going to get in line for the lift and head on up there. Any questions?"

We pushed over to where all the chairs came in for a landing. Drew talked to the guy who was standing next to the control box, and then turned to us.

"This thing doesn't stop. So you have to get on and off pretty quickly," Drew instructed. "Keep your feet up and be ready to jump off. It goes faster than it looks, so I want you paying attention. Okay, Ryan will make sure you get on all right, so I can be there when you get off. See you at the top!" He jumped on the first seat and started up the mountain.

The striped-hat couple went first. Then Molly and her dad. Before I had time to think, Liz grabbed my hand and pulled me forward. I wanted to tell her wait, I had to tie my bootlace, or Margie was waiting for me back at the chalet, but I didn't have time, because all of a sudden the earth was falling away from us and we were lifting into the air.

I heard myself howl.

"Pretty cool, right?" said Liz.

"Sure," I squeaked. I was trying to do that special breathing I learned on Mom's yoga tape, but I sounded like I was about to give birth to an elephant.

"Wahoo!" yelled Liz, totally oblivious to our impending doom. "Now remember, it's not going to stop, so get ready," she warned. And then the mountaintop was coming toward us and I saw Drew's orange goggles and the striped-hat couple standing with their arms around each other, watching us come in.

"Keep your feet out!" yelled Drew, as the ground got closer and closer.

"Wheeeeeee!" squealed Liz, sailing out ahead of me.

"Go, Sam, go!" called Drew. I closed my eyes and pitched myself forward, my stomach flipping up into my chest. My skis went out in either direction and my butt started sinking. And then there were two hands on my waist, steering me forward, slowly, securely.

"Atta girl," said Drew into my ear. "You got it."

We came to a stop and he turned me around. "Nice job," he said, but I was panting too hard to respond. "Pretty cool, huh?" he said with a wink, and then squeezed my shoulder. Man, this guy was slick. I saw Heidi and Dina watching the whole thing, whispering into each other's ears.

The rest of the group came in. Even Molly had a smoother landing than me. *But she's closer to the ground, so it's easier for her, right?* Then Drew led us over a little ways to what he called the Junior Slope. Only, it didn't look too junior to me. It was pretty much a straight shot down to the bottom — no trees or anything to break the fall. The chalet looked like it was worlds away. My knees felt like loose noodles, and my heart was pounding in my ears. Was there a way to take that chairlift back down instead?

"Okay, now we're going to have some fun," said Drew. "Remember, you're going to keep your head up, maintain your center of gravity," he said. "And keep your behind —"

"*Behind!*" answered the rest of the group. I wanted to laugh because it was so corny, but I still couldn't spare the air.

Zoom! went the striped hats.

Zoom! went Liz. *Zoom! Zoom!* Dina and Heidi. I could hear them laughing and hollering the whole way down. Molly and her dad went next. No fatalities so far. *Come on, Levy, you can do this.* But every time I looked over the edge, I felt frozen and my knees buckled. I tried digging my poles into the snow, and they kept slipping out to the sides.

Then Drew was by my side, plowing to a stop.

"You need a hand?" He flashed me one of his dazzling smiles.

"Yeah, I guess so," I muttered, looking back at the ground.

"First, make sure you have a firm grip on these things." He gave me the poles and then laid his gloved hands over my mittens.

"Next, I want you to put your weight forward, like you're almost going to tip over." He leaned his body into my back. "You okay?" he murmured. He was so close to my ear I could almost feel the words coming off his tongue.

"Yeah," I managed to say. It wasn't just the air now that was making me dizzy. This was definitely the closest I'd ever been to a guy — without being onstage battling the great Dust Bowl, that is.

"You think you're ready to give it a go?"

"Yeah, sure," I swallowed. "I'm just a little slow."

"Fine by me. I've got all day," he said. His hands were still on top of mine. I could hear him breathing behind me.

"But maybe all you really need is a *push*!" And with that Drew grabbed my waist and shoved me forward.

The ground started sliding out from under me.

"Aaaaahgh!" I was shrieking.

"Don't forget to bend your knees!" I heard him call. But everything was moving too fast. It was just a rush of snow and trees and the sky swirling past. The wind was whipping my face and I was tipping forward and then back.

I heard someone shouting, "Slow down, Sam! Slow down!" and I looked out and it was Liz coming toward me faster and faster. And I was trying to move my feet together to make that T with my skis but they kept on moving forward, forward, and now I was trying to pull them together, I needed them to meet in the middle, but they were still racing straight ahead, no matter what I did.

"T-stop! T-stop!" Liz was yelling. At this point, that was about as helpful as yelling at me that the sky was blue. Which it was, and it was coming down toward me now, or else I was going up. And then my feet were in the air and so were my poles and I knew this wasn't right but I wasn't sure how to fix it and I was headed for a big pile of snow. *Leeeeeevyyyyyyy!*

Chapter 4

It wasn't that bad. It could've been much worse. I was on my back. My skis were both sticking out of the ground. My poles were somewhere around here. Nothing really hurt, except for my butt a little. And my pride.

"Wow," said Liz, standing over me.

Heidi and Dina were right behind her, peering anxiously at me. The striped hats were keeping their distance. Molly's dad lifted her onto his shoulders so she could get a better view.

"Whoa, looks like somebody likes to fly," said Drew. He came to a stop next to me, the snow spraying my legs. "You okay?" he asked.

"Yeah, sorry."

"No need to apologize. I was the one who pushed you. Do you hate me?" He pulled up his goggles and his blue eyes twinkled.

"No," I said.

"Good. Because we're gonna get back up there and try that again. You and me." He gave a little nod, then grabbed my wrist and lifted me up with one hand.

"Okay, circle up, folks," said Drew.

Everyone came into a huddle at the bottom of the Junior Slope.

"A few notes. Erica and Andrew, nice form." The striped hats nodded. "Liz — you could bend your knees more. Especially when you're making some of those weight shifts. Remember, folks, this is going to give you more stability when you want to do things in the future like go through trees, or try moguls."

What are moguls?

"Got it," said Liz confidently.

Drew continued. "Dina, nice work, I like your plow stop. Heidi, you can loosen up your grip on the poles a little." Neither of them looked up. "And Molly, you are the all-time champion! Did you guys see this? You're like the fastest one here! That's what I'm talking about!"

He took off his glove and gave her tiny pink mitten

a high five. She was smiling so wide I thought she would split in half.

"And that leaves us with just . . . you."

His finger was long and pointed straight at me. But there was a smile sneaking up his face.

"We're going to have to do a little tutorial. One-on-one," he said.

We headed back to the chairlift, and Drew went up first. Erica and Andrew sat in the next one.

"Come on, Sam. The next one is ours," said Liz. We slid into the seats and raised our feet in front of us. The car started floating up. *Okay, take it slow, Levy. 1, 2, inhale. 1, 2, exhale.*

"Wow, pretty awesome!" said Liz.

"Yeah, it feels like the air is cleaner up here. Lighter," I said.

"Yeah, whatever," Liz laughed. "I wasn't talking about the air. I was talking about you and Super G having a private lesson." She nudged me in the ribs.

"Super G?"

"That's what Heidi and Dina and I call him. Did you see Heidi when he told you about your one-on-one time?" She giggled again. "I thought she was gonna melt into a puddle!"

"Uh, well. I mean, she can join us, if she wants. It's just 'cause I can't walk up the stairs without tripping."

Liz rolled her eyes. "I don't *think* so, Sam. Aren't you excited?"

I shrugged.

"Sam, he is a total hottie! And he's been to the Olympics!"

"What is the Super G, anyway?" I asked.

"Who cares?! The point is, he's super dreamy and he obviously wants to get to know you. Are you seeing someone or something?"

Now it was my turn to laugh. Should I mention Leo and *The Grapes of Wrath*?

"No but —I don't know. He's not really my type."

"What do you mean?" Liz asked, clearly confused.

"I don't know. I guess I like guys who are . . . who are . . ." What? I thought of that cute guy Aaron from lunch. Incommunicative? Leo. Unavailable?

"Well, all I can say is that I know plenty of girls who would die to be in your position. He looks like an awesome kisser, too. Can you imagine looking into those eyes? You should've seen Heidi and Dina this morning during class."

"Well, if *they* like him —"

"Nah, don't worry about it. Heidi gets a new crush every other day. And Dina has been seeing the same guy for, like, five months. It's really serious. I wouldn't be surprised if they got married."

"Well, what about you?"

"I won't lie. I was pretty smitten, too. That is, until lunch." Her voice got softer now and I froze. Oh, no. Did she think Aaron was cute, too? I heard her take in a breath. "So, is your brother seeing anyone?"

Ew! It took all my energy not to squirm. Or yell, "Run! Run for the hills!" Instead I said, "Hmmm, I don't think so."

"*Really*," Liz murmured.

There was so much swimming in my head all at once now. Leo and Aaron and Jeremy and Drew. Drew?! Could he really be interested in *me*? I tried to imagine myself strolling into Dave Murphy's basement with Drew, his Olympic medal swinging around his neck. I wondered if he knew how to play Murder.

"Sam! Get ready!" Liz was saying. And there was Molly and her dad waving at us wildly. And behind them Drew was giving us the thumbs-up. *All right, Levy, get it together this time.*

"Now!" Liz commanded.

We flew off and landed. I wobbled my way to a stop.

"Yeah! Nice!" I heard. Drew came over and patted me on the back. Liz smiled and then bugged out her eyes at me.

Drew gathered us together up at the top of Junior Slope again and then instructed everyone to take it slow, watch their center of gravity, and most of all, have fun.

Once the rest of the group had taken off, he led me to another little area, just past some trees. Then he turned to face me.

"Now, let's get down to business."

He started to unzip his jacket. What?! Was this really happening? Agh! What do I do?! *Think fast, Levy. Think fast!* I looked at the ground quickly.

"I swear I go through like three of these a week," I heard him say.

Huh?

He had a cherry-flavored ChapStick in his hand, and he was smearing it onto his lips. He was also zipping up a pocket inside his jacket.

I let out a breath. *Levy, you're such a nut job. Yeah, like he was going to strip down to his boxers and try to bed you here on the Junior Slope summit*. I started to laugh a little. I couldn't help it.

"I know. I know. A guy using cherry ChapStick. Whatever. But it really is the best kind and otherwise your lips get so chapped," he said.

"No, no! I use the same kind. Sometimes," I said. This was painful.

He flashed another smile. "You want some?"

He had just put some on his lips. And then I was going to put some on my lips. Which was like our lips coming together. Which was —

"Sam?"

"Oh, yeah. Sure, thanks." I took the ChapStick like it was no big deal and put some on.

"Now listen," he said, zipping up his jacket again. "It's all gonna be about using your knees. Really getting close to your center of gravity, which is down here." He patted his stomach. Then he reached out and put his hand in the middle of my jacket, just below my ribs.

"You feel that?" he said.

"Yup," I said. *Definitely,* I added to myself.

"Okay, so you're gonna always want to stay low to the ground and really bend into it. Got it?"

I nodded.

"Now, we have to loosen your body up. You're still

really stiff," he said. He started shaking my shoulders side to side, jiggling my arms.

That's probably because I'm sixteen and I've never really been kissed by a guy and Liz said you were interested, but are you really? I mean, because you are definitely the hottest guy I've ever met, but I've never really been into hot guys before and I don't want you to just take pity on me because I have flat hair and a turtle hat and I think my breath smells like French fries and I don't even know if you read books or recycle or you could eat babies for all I know!

Drew had his hands on my hips.

"Now, lean into it. Move my hands back and forth."

I swayed my hips from side to side. It looked more like hula dancing than skiing, but whatever, right? We worked on braking and stopping. Drew was really serious now, studying my feet, watching my knees. He had me do a couple of practice runs on a little dip. It wasn't even a hill, but I still managed to teeter and fall a few times.

"The knees, Sam! It's all in the knees!" he urged. He sounded kind of frustrated. I was thinking of telling him it was okay. That there were plenty of other books at the inn. I'd find something to do for the rest of the week. There had to be a deck of cards somewhere.

And then, it just clicked. Or unclicked. I don't know. But one time, I guess when I wasn't thinking about it so much, my body kind of let go. Instead of gripping so hard, I felt like I was loosening into it.

"Yeah! That's what I'm talking about!" Drew said when I came to a stop. Ew. There was that phrase again. There's a whole bunch of guys at school who hang out in the parking lot and say that to girls they think are cute. Not my favorite. But I tried not to wince.

Drew and I practiced glides and turns, leaning into one ski and then the other. How to add speed. What to do when you felt like you were going too fast. It was really fun. I don't know how long we were up there, and I didn't care. My cheeks felt bright and cold, my thighs were burning from doing so many squats. It was really invigorating.

"And now . . . it is time for takeoff," Drew announced. He flipped his goggles down over his eyes. "You ready, doll?"

Doll? I had to laugh at that one. That was a word that old Italian men used when you bought a pound of turkey breast at the deli, right? Was this guy for real?

"I guess," I said.

We made our way back to the edge of the Junior

Slope. It still looked big, but my legs felt strong. Drew leaned in behind me and whispered into my ear, "I'm not pushing this time, Sam. It's all you. Keep your behind *behind*."

Still cheesy. But he was a professional. I needed to respect that.

I drew in a deep breath, bent my knees, gripped my poles, and then before I could talk myself out of it, pushed off. I leaned forward and squatted down farther, tucking my butt behind me. *Focus. Relax. Focus. Don't think too much.* And I was doing it! I could feel the earth moving below me, and the wind was carrying me and I picked up my poles like Drew had taught me and now I was really moving. I saw a little mound of snow up ahead of me and I leaned into my right ski and gently shifted past it, then steadied myself again. The clouds were soaring past and I felt my heart racing, the sun on my face, my nose cutting through the cold. And my legs were shifting, leaning, dancing, alive.

"Yeah!" I heard Drew behind me.

When I got to the bottom, I came to a clean stop, the snow spraying away from my skis in a lopsided-but-okay-it'll-pass-for-a-T.

Drew flew in after me.

"Now, *that* is what I am talking *about*!" he cheered. Hey, when it came with one of those killer smiles, I'd take it.

And then he pulled me into a hug. His grip was so strong and tight, I could barely breathe.

Wait — was he holding me? Was I officially in the arms of Drew McHottie?

"I knew you could do it, girl! Come on, let's go again!" he said, and he grabbed my hand, pushing off toward the chairlift.

The rest of that afternoon was a blur of treetops and wind, dips and turns. We took the Junior Slope another two times, and then Drew led me to an area called Powder Ridge that had steeper inclines, a couple of curves, and small patches of trees. When we got to the bottom of that one, we found Jeremy, Aaron, and Liz.

"Hey!" said Liz, her face flushed and bright.

"Hey!" I said back, still panting from the last run.

"Did you see Sam attack that mountain?" said Drew, lifting my arm up.

"Yeah. Hey, nice job, Sam," said Liz. "We were thinking of going in to get some hot chocolate. You wanna come?"

Hot chocolate sounded perfect right now, but I didn't want to lose my momentum.

"Yeah, I could go for a cup," said Drew.

We all headed in.

"Hiya, kids! How'd you do?" said Dad. He and Kathy were sitting by the fire with — yup, none other than Margie. Dad looked super excited to see us. Kathy jumped up, too, and gave Jeremy a big smile, but was still avoiding my eyes. Ugh. I had conveniently forgotten about that situation for the past few hours. Now, who was being the baby?

Everybody made introductions. Margie, Drew, Liz, Aaron, Jeremy, Dad. *My new wife, Kathy.* It stung when he said it.

"Well, what do you say we call it a day?" said Dad. "We're kinda beat." He kissed Kathy on top of her head.

"Well, wait. What are you all doing tonight?" asked Liz. "I know Dina and Heidi and I would be up for going out if you wanna . . . ?" She was looking right at Jeremy while she said it. Yow. This girl was direct. Jeremy, of course, just stared back blankly.

"I could go for an evening activity," Drew offered.

And then Kathy said, "Hey, I saw they're having

karaoke around eight-thirty tonight where we're staying. I don't know if that's your thing, but I'm sure you folks could come over. Judd here could give you directions to the inn." She looked at Dad.

He nodded his head proudly. "Sure could," he said.

"I love karaoke!" said Liz, practically jumping out of her skin. "I think we're staying right near you, so that'll be great!" She smiled up at Jeremy with her sparkle-dusted eyes. Jeremy still looked pretty unmoved. But hey — what was I expecting? This was the guy who only showed emotion about the NFL draft season and frozen pizza pockets.

"You in?" he said to Aaron.

"I'm not sure. Gotta check with the other guys, but maybe," he said. Noncommittal, too. Usual Levy fare. And he still hadn't even looked at me long enough to see if I had horns. Then I felt Drew's hands on my shoulders.

"Well, I'm not much of a singer, but I love to make a fool out of myself," he said behind me. Which was good because then I didn't have to look at him. I didn't have to say, *What are you doing?* Or, *Do you do this with all the klutzes?* Or, *Why can't you be more like Aaron — aloof, uninterested, and in bad need of a hairstyle?* Or maybe, *Have you ever read* Catcher in the Rye? Agh! I needed to get back to the inn and call Phoebe *now.*

"Well, it's pretty easy to get to," said Dad. "It's called Bishop Inn and it's off of Route —"

"Yeah, Bishop Inn. I know where that is. I've been there before," said Drew.

Liz looked at me and raised an eyebrow. What did *that* mean?

"Okay. Well then, eight-thirty!" she said.

"Yeah," said Drew, and now he was definitely looking right at me. "I'll be there."

Chapter 5

"Can I say something?" Jeremy had his mouth full of toothpaste and he looked like a rabid dog foaming at the mouth.

"Only if it's nice," I said, stepping away from the full-length mirror. I knew I should have closed the bathroom door when I was done in there.

"That's the fifth sweater you've tried on, and they all look the same."

"They do not!" I objected, even though I knew he was right. It was pointless. Everything I had to wear was either gray or black, except for the one dark green turtleneck sweater, but that made me look like a Christmas tree without the colored lights or tinsel.

"Just wear what you had on the first time," said Jeremy, spitting into the sink. Of course he would say that. He had no idea what the first thing I tried on was. All of my sweaters lay in a heap on the bed.

I had no one to blame but myself. I remembered packing at home the week before, complaining the whole time. Mom was sitting in my desk chair with a cup of mint tea, her legs tucked up under her.

"Aren't you going to take a skirt or two? Something nice in case you want to get dressed up?"

"I'll have what I wore to the wedding," I groaned. Which was a tight black skirt that came to my knees and a black velvet V-neck. I looked like I was going to a funeral. It was also 68 degrees in Orlando. That outfit was on the bed now, too.

"Listen, I'll meet you down there," said Jeremy from the bathroom.

"No!" I shot back. Jeremy had it easy, with deep-set eyes — just like Mom's — and his thick, dark curls. Why did he get the good hair? Even when it was dirty, it made sense. He just put some water on his face and he was ready to go. Like now, he was wearing the same jeans and striped thermal top that he had on this morning, but it didn't matter.

"Just give me two more minutes," I pleaded. "Rearrange your freckles or something."

"Two minutes. That's it," he said. I heard him flop down on the bed and turn on professional wrestling. At least he was easily distracted.

I put on the velvet V-neck and my low-rider jeans. Sexy? No. What had Phoebe said when we spoke on the phone before? *Sassy?*

Wait.

First she said, "Aaaaaaaagh! Sam, that is so exciting!"

"Yeah, I don't know. He's superhot. But he's also super-cheesy. Like, did I tell you he called me 'doll'? And he wears those nylon pants that swish all the time?"

"Sam, he's a *skier*. They have to wear nylon. It's in their contract or something. And he was in the *Olympics*," she said.

"Just the trials," I corrected.

"Whatever, Miss Judgy McJudgealot."

"I don't know, it's just . . ."

"Sam, this is what we have been talking about. You need to get out there! See what guys are like. *Real guys*."

"Yeah, and there's this other guy named Aaron. But

he doesn't talk much. And he kind of hunches over and his shoulders are really bony," I said.

"Wow. Door number one, please," said Phoebe.

"Yeah, but he could be really sweet," I protested.

"You can have him," said Phoebe. "I'll take Drew — oh, I wish I was there," she sighed.

"I do, too. Hey, how was Bonnie Briar?"

"Boo. Nothing happened. There were too many people around. Rachel and I were on one of those saucer sleddy things, and Leo and Josh kept on crashing into us."

"Leo?" I said. I didn't mean it to come out quite so whimpery.

"Oh, come on, Sam. Please don't tell me you are up in a winter wonderland with Super G Hotness and you are still thinking about Leo Strumm?"

"No, but —"

"Listen, girl. You put on something sassy and some jewelry and mascara and get down to that karaoke machine. What are you gonna sing?"

I hadn't even thought about that yet. My heart was racing already.

"Don't worry about it. Get a standard, like Madonna

or something. And just close your eyes if you have to and belt it out. Oooh! I wish I could see you," she squealed. This would definitely be more fun if Phoebe was here with me. Forty-five minutes later, here I was, sighing into the mirror again.

"You done?" called Jeremy.

"Almost!"

The V-neck made me look really flat-chested. Ah, who was I kidding? I *was* pretty flat-chested. And pale. Mom always told me to put blush on, but I hated that. Instead, I pulled out my little tube of shimmery gel and squeezed out a blob. Then I rubbed some into my chest and above my eyes. Great. Now I looked like a sparkly ghost.

I searched my duffel for some jewelry. I knew there was a simple silver star I had tucked into the inside pocket.

"Time's up!" Jeremy was in the doorway again.

"Here, Jer, can you help me?"

But when I turned toward him, he was already busy.

"Ew! Don't pick your nose! That's gross, Jeremy!"

"It's not gross! It's natural!"

Poor Liz. She had no idea what she was in for.

By the time we got downstairs, Karaoke Night was already in full swing. We followed the music through the dining area into another room, this one with a fireplace in the middle and those floor-to-ceiling windows on three sides. On the fourth side, there was a small platform, where Phil now stood.

"Stevie D. is up next. Calling to the stage Stevie D.," announced Phil. Stevie D. was the Hawaiian-looking guy I had seen the other day. Only now he had a raccoon-eye tan from his ski goggles, and a big grin as he came up to grab the microphone.

"This one's for you, Dara," he said, and started in with Frank Sinatra's "I've Got You Under My Skin." The crowd started humming underneath him.

The woman who must have been Dara sat two feet away, looking up at Stevie D. and mouthing all the words along with him.

I looked around. There were couches pushed to the edges of the room and little card tables set up with votive candles. Dad and Kathy were seated with another couple in the corner. I sincerely hoped they didn't plan on staying long. There was a family of four next to them — two boys that looked to be between eight and maybe twelve. Both looking incredibly bored.

And in the center of it all was Drew. There were two seats between him and Liz. Then came Dina and Heidi, who was sitting really close to some new guy I had never met before. He had spiky hair, too, and a little goatee. Wait — wasn't she all giggly about Drew just this afternoon? She *did* move fast. And I guess Aaron hadn't made it. Which somehow didn't surprise me really. What surprised me was that I was fine with that. My eyes were still caught on Drew. His hair was carefully tousled, his face glowing in the light of the tiny flame. He was wearing a dark sweater that outlined the shape of his broad shoulders, and he was holding a glass of something clear and chewing on an ice cube. I watched as the muscles in his jaw moved up and down.

"Hello, Darth Vader," said Jeremy, elbowing me in the side.

I was taking deep, loud breaths through my mouth. I do that whenever I'm really nervous. I shut my mouth quickly. *Get it together, Levy.*

Liz looked up and waved us over, pointing to two empty seats in between her and Drew. By now, everyone was singing, "'Cause I've got you, under my skin!" Jeremy and I snuck over and slid into the chairs.

"Hey!" said Liz, grinning ear to ear.

"Hey!" I said back.

"Hey," said Jeremy.

And then "Hey," Drew whispered into my hair.

Stay cool, Levy. Stay cool.

"Let's give it up for Stevie D.! Stevie D., all the way here from Maui," said Phil.

Stevie took a bow and was greeted with a big kiss from Dara.

"And next up we have Illona. Illona from Little Rock, Arkansas. I'm sure you'll all like this one she's picked for you. Let's hear it for Ben E. King's 'Stand By Me.'" Jeez, the selection here seemed like pretty old stuff. But I didn't care. I wasn't planning on singing. I was just concentrating on breathing through my nose right now and feeling Drew's nearness.

After Illona went up, Dad and Kathy did a duet by Kenny Rogers and Dolly Parton — "Islands in the Stream." Barf city. Especially because Kathy knew all the words by heart and was gazing up at Dad the whole time with this moony look in her eyes. But I was determined not to let her ruin my night. I shoved four pieces of gum in my mouth and tried to chomp out my tension, being careful to keep my mouth closed.

Then Liz shoved the book of songs at me. She had found a section called NEW ADDITIONS! at the back of the book. She pointed to a song by a Canadian singer named Hailey Burke — "Lost and Found." I loved that song. It was on her second album that had just come out, and Phoebe and I both had it. When nobody was home, we just put it on repeat and danced and sang at the top of our lungs. But that was different than doing it here in front of everybody. Especially in front of Drew.

Liz's eyes were shiny and wild. I looked at her, with her turquoise off-the-shoulder sweater, her blond hair tumbling down her back in soft waves, and gold hoops dangling from her ears. She had on matching turquoise eye shadow and her cheeks were glowing.

"Pleeeaase?" said Liz, coquettishly. "We'll all be up there together, Sam."

Heidi and Dina leaned in, too. "Come on, Sam! It'll be fun!"

Dina had on a creamy-looking sweater poncho, and Heidi was in a clingy red sweater dress. These girls knew how to sass it up. And probably knew how to sing, too. I didn't want to be the only lame-o who wasn't singing. Mostly because Phoebe would kill me when I reported back to her later. I shrugged my shoulders. Liz took it as a yes.

"Yay! I'm putting you in," she said, and sashayed

her way up to Phil with a slip of paper that had our names on it. Dina and Heidi clapped and cheered, "Yay!"

Before I could protest, Dad and Kathy were standing over our table, both beaming.

Oh, no! Please don't make me and Jeremy do a number with you. We are not the Von Trapp family. Please please please please please.

"Did you see what Kathy made me do up there?" said Dad, pulling her into his hip.

"I didn't *make* you, Judd!" she giggled and squirmed. I wished I hadn't bitten off all of my nails that morning with Margie. At least Margie was more interesting than Ricecake.

"I thought you sounded great up there, Mr. and Mrs. Levy," said Dina carefully.

I was just about to jump out of my seat and yell, "No! That is *not* Mr. and Mrs. Levy!" but Dad must've sensed it because he blurted out really quickly, "All right, kids. Well, that's enough fun for one day. Us old folks are headin' upstairs. See you in the morning for another run at that mountain!" And then he swung around with Kathy still attached to his hip.

"Have fun!" said Kathy, tucking her hand in Dad's back pocket as they walked away.

"Your mom's really smiley," said Drew.

Sorry, but that was too much.

"*Not* my mom," I snapped.

"Whoa. O-kay," he said, reaching for his glass. Jeremy just shook his head.

Liz came back with a devilish grin on her face. "We're in!" she announced, smoothing out her corduroy miniskirt.

Some guy in a loose flannel shirt and jeans was up there now, singing a Billy Joel song. He was horribly off-key and he wouldn't take his eyes off the screen. Poor dude. That was going to be me in just a few minutes. I wanted to catch laryngitis. Or maybe I could burn myself slightly on the candle . . . ?

Then Phil took the mike. "Next up, we have Liz, Heidi, and —"

He didn't even get to finish calling our names before the girls were up on their feet, skipping to the front of the room.

"Go get 'em, girl!" rumbled Drew, and then he squeezed my knee.

Liz got on the microphone. "Sam, to the front of the room. Sam, please report to the front of the room."

Great. Just what I needed. More attention. *Get up,*

Levy! I smushed my wad of gum into a napkin and walked to the front of the room with my head down. I tried to hide myself behind Dina, but she was a good three inches or so shorter than me. Story of my life.

The music started. First the violins. Then the piano. Then:

You were lost
In the shadow of a tree
Under a rock
Right next to me

Liz's voice was firm and sweet. She swayed her hips from side to side. Damn, she was good. Dina and Heidi followed in line. I could hear Dina warbling a little, but she kept going. The drums kicked in underneath, then the piano. Heidi punched me on the arm. Well, when in Rome . . .

I'm learning, every day
How to saaaaaaaaaaaaaaaaay

I wasn't exactly smooth like the other girls, but I tried to just focus on the lyrics. I thought of Hailey in the video, singing as she walked through a wide-open field. Then I pictured myself and Phoebe spinning on her living room floor in our socks. I could do this. As long as I didn't look out at all those faces. I closed my eyes and just let the music take over my body.

You're beautiful, yes it's true
And I'll never let you go now that I've found you
I've found youuuuuuuuu

And now I could feel my shoulders draw back, and the lights on my cheeks, my voice melting into Hailey's and Liz's and . . . I couldn't believe it but I was doing it! If Phoebe could see me now!

When the song ended, Drew jumped to his feet, hooting and whistling. "Now, that's what I'm talking about!" he yelled. I could feel my face turning crimson.

"Encore!" yelled the guy with the goatee, standing up, too.

"Thanks, folks. We'll be here all night. Seriously, we love you," said Liz, blowing a kiss to the audience. More applause. I didn't know where or how Liz got her confidence, but it sure was awesome. I was starting to really like her. We made our way back to our seats. Drew was still standing up, clapping.

"Did we do okay?" asked Liz, looking right at Jeremy.

"Yeah, it was fun," he said blandly. My brother, the romantic.

"You looked *fine,* ladies!" said Drew. I was too embarassed to look at him. Then he turned to the guy next to Heidi and said, "Hey, Trey. You wanna do this?"

"Sure."

"Do what?" asked Liz.

"Well, Trey and I brought some stuff so we could go outside in the hot tub and party a little," said Drew.

Hot tub? There was a hot tub here? How did they know that?

"What kind of stuff?" asked Heidi with a giggle.

"You know, my friend Jack D," said Drew, tipping an imaginary bottle back into his mouth.

"But we didn't bring any stuff to *wear,*" moaned Dina.

"I've got a couple of pairs of boxers and some T-shirts in my bag," said Drew. "You've got some, too, right, T?"

"Yup."

"You guys have towels in your rooms, I assume?" Drew asked me and Jeremy.

"Yeah," said Jeremy. I wondered if he was thinking what I was thinking. The two of us in a hot tub. Together. Wasn't that a little ooky? And ever since the cast party at Dave's, I'd been pretty nervous around alcohol. I'd never even tasted whiskey.

"Sounds like a plan to me!" said Liz eagerly.

What was I going to do, chicken out and go upstairs to watch more reality TV by myself? *C'mon, Levy. Don't be a total loser.* This was winter break. This was feeling sexy and sassy and learning how to live a little.

"Whaddaya say, dollface?" asked Drew. All right, we'd need to work on the lingo a little, but . . .

"I'm in."

Jeremy led the way as we tried to duck out around the back of the room. Stevie D. was already on the mike again, this time with a Barry Manilow song. Talk about cheesy.

Then, just as I was turning to head out through the open archway, I saw a figure in a chair in the corner, his head bent over what looked like a large pad of paper, his hand scribbling. Was that . . . ?

Eric, Phil's son, looked up and turned the pad over quickly.

"Hey," he said.

"Hey."

"Nice work up there," he told me, nodding at the stage.

"Oh, that? That was stupid."

"Why? I thought it was pretty good."

"Whatever," I said. The candle flickered in front of him and I could see there was a smudge of charcoal on his lower lip. Neither of us said anything.

"What are you doing back here all alone?" I said finally. I didn't mean it to sound that rude, but I guess I still wasn't a big fan of the guy.

"Just — nothing."

"Must be something."

"Drawing," he said. And he pulled the pad closer to his chest.

"Huh?"

"Drawing. You know, like sketching? I sketch sometimes."

"Really? In the dark?"

"This is fine." He lifted up the tea light and gave a kind of crooked smile.

"Oh."

"So, did you go skiing today?" he asked.

"Yeah."

"How'd it go?"

"Good I guess. By the end I was doing okay."

"Drew was your teacher?" How did this guy know — agh! Drew!

"Yeah, actually, you know what? I gotta go!" I felt really nervous and excited, but mostly nervous now, and a little mad at myself. Why was I still talking to this guy, anyway? I mean it was sad that he was alone and all, but I had to get upstairs. Now!

I raced through the dining room and then into the lobby. The fire was giving its last licks and the armchairs were empty. I skipped past them and took the stairs two at a time. Made it to the top, too! And then promptly tripped over the Oriental rug lying there, in typical Levy fashion.

Chapter 6

By the time I got up to the room, everyone was changed into T-shirts and boxers. Heidi had her hair up in two cute ponytails, and Liz had tied her T-shirt into a knot just above her smooth belly. Dina came out of the bathroom wearing a baby tee that she must've had under her sweater that had a picture of a cat on it. I could tell she wasn't wearing a bra, either. The guys were on the bed, passing a bottle of Jack Daniel's.

"There she is!" said Drew, raising the bottle toward me.

"We were just gonna come downstairs to find you!" said Liz.

Jeremy handed me a worn-out T-shirt that said

DYSPEPSIA: DEADLY? NO. UNCOMFORTABLE? YES. and a pair of plaid boxers. Not exactly sexy, but I didn't have much choice. All I had brought were thermals. I said thanks and headed to the bathroom.

"Sam, honey, do you mind if we head out there? We're just really excited to get in!" called Liz.

"Sure!" I called back. Phoebe would never leave me like that. *But hey, time to start growing up, Levy.*

"Don't be too long, Sammygirl," came Drew's deep voice.

I slipped into the T-shirt and shorts and then looked in the mirror.

"Okay," I said to my reflection. I rubbed a little more lip gloss on and then mashed my lips into the back of my hand, just for a practice run. It left a glossy circle on my skin.

"Nerd," I whispered to myself, and then giggled under my breath.

Then I leaned in closer. Pimple still underground. Check. Eyebrows plucked. Check. Freckles in line. Check. Go time.

Downstairs, I tiptoed across the back of the living room. Dara was up there now singing Bette Midler's "Wind Beneath My Wings." Stevie D. was standing up, singing just inches from her face. Besides that, it looked pretty empty. I was careful not to look in the corner, in case Eric was still sitting there in the dark.

I pulled open the sliding door. Yeesh! My whole body trembled as my bare skin met the air. It was *much* colder outside once the sun went down.

"Psst! Over here!" giggled Heidi.

Her voice drifted over from behind a line of snow-covered bushes just past a covered pool. I guessed they used this place all year-round. It was hard to imagine it without a blanket of snow.

"Hey! Pass it over! No hogging, Liz!" said Dina playfully.

I turned the corner behind the hedge and there were six figures rising out of a cloud of steam with lights shining up, making them look like they were an alien spaceship that had just landed.

"Come on in, Sam, the water's fine!" said Liz, lifting the bottle to her lips.

Drew put out his hand and I stepped in carefully. The water felt hot and bubbly and I was glad I kept my bra on because my shirt floated up to the surface when I lowered down. Then I slid down next to Drew on a tiled bench that went all around the tub.

"Want some?" asked Liz. She held the bottle out over the water.

"I do!" called Dina. "Wait, is anyone gonna come out here and check on us?"

"Nah, they don't care," said Drew. "Besides, aren't you legal?" He raised his eyebrows with a sly smile.

"I'll be sixteen next month!" she twittered.

"I'm gonna be seventeen!" said Liz proudly. "How about you?" she said, obviously to Jeremy.

"Eighteen."

"Sixteen," said Heidi, nudging Trey.

"Seventeen," he said, tickling her.

"Eighteen," said Drew.

"Sixteen," I said. "Almost." Ugh. I couldn't lie, though.

"Here, Sam. You want some?" Dina handed me the whiskey bottle.

"Yeah, sure." I felt all eyes on me as I touched the cold glass up to my teeth and then slowly tipped it into my mouth. It felt warm and smooth, sliding down my throat, leaving a soft burn in my belly. It was actually pretty nice.

"You okay?" Jeremy asked.

"Sure, why?" I said, shrugging. I hoped he wasn't

going to be checking in with me all night. I could take care of myself. I quickly took another swig.

"That's what I'm talking about!" said Drew, taking the bottle from me.

We passed it around again. I watched the steam swirling around in the center of the tub. The night felt magical, the moon a soft slip, carved into the endless sky, surrounded in a misty halo.

"Hey, I have an idea! Let's play truth or dare!" said Liz. Her eyes glinted in the moonlight. She was looking directly at Jeremy.

Jeremy looked at me. I didn't know what to say, but I guess my face said it all, because he said, "I think that might be a little weird for Sam and me."

"Riiiiiight," said Liz, smiling.

"How about twenty questions?" said Heidi.

"Okay!" said Dina.

"What's that?" asked Drew.

"Yeah, what's that?" echoed Trey.

"Easy," said Liz. "All right. I'm thinking of a person, place, or thing. You have twenty questions you can ask to guess what it is. Ready? Go!"

When the bottle came back to me I took a long sip, and this time when it slipped down into my stomach I could feel my limbs grow lighter and bubbly. I handed the bottle to Drew.

"Thank you, madam," he said in his deep, delicious voice, and now everything was swaying a little bit and a giggle escaped from my lips.

"Animal, vegetable, or mineral?" I asked, popping up.

"Animal! That's one," said Liz.

"Jeez, it's cold out here!" I ducked back down until the water was up to my chin. My arms looked like spaghetti sticks underneath.

"You can sit here and I'll keep you warm," said Drew. He pulled me toward him and sat me in between his legs on the little bench. I felt his hands running up and down my arms, and my chest pounding.

"Thanks," I chirped.

"You still cold, rock star?" he murmured, his breath tickling my cheek.

"Nope!" I managed, my voice higher still. *Be cool, Levy. Be cool. And whatever you do, don't look at your brother.*

"Nobody's guessing!" complained Liz, but she was still smiling.

"Is it a person?" asked Dina.

"Yes, sort of."

"How can it *sort of* be a person?" asked Heidi.

"Keep guessing!"

The bottle came around again. I grabbed it greedily, felt the warm rush of it travel down my throat.

"Is it George Bush?" said Drew. I could feel his voice rumbling in my back.

"No."

"Is it Harry Potter?" I said. My words were sliding into each other.

"No."

"Is it God?"

I remembered my little prayer from the night before. Boy, a lot had changed in a few short hours. Now I had an Olympic skier with the most amazing blue eyes holding me, and the sky was so huge it went on forever, and the stars were circling, and everything was gently revolving around me. I didn't care about Kathy now, or Leo, or . . . what was his name? Oh, yeah. Aaron. The moon felt closer to me than all of them now.

"Okay, I'll give you a hint," said Liz. "He's Indian."

"Ooh! I know!" cried Heidi. "Is it Mahatma Gundy?"

And then we were all laughing.

"*Gundy?*" yelped Liz, between cackles.

"You know what I meant!" said Heidi, but she was laughing, too.

"I know what you said!"

It wasn't even that funny. But I couldn't stop laughing, and it was so great to hear our voices dancing up into the night, bouncing off the trees, fading into the darkness. I felt Drew's arms holding me tighter now. His breath in my hair.

My hair. Me. Sam Levy. Super-dweeb.

"But who was it really?" asked Jeremy after he caught his breath.

"What? Oh, Buddha!"

"Yoga freak!" cried Dina.

"Pat the belly! Pat the belly!" said Liz, and we all laughed again.

"Who's gonna finish this off?" said Drew, holding the bottle up over my head. The light from the bottom of the hot tub came through the brown liquid and it sparkled.

"Ooh, me!" said Dina and I at the same time. I reached my arms up, even though my whole body got goose bumps, but Drew pulled the bottle just out of reach.

"No fighting, ladies. There's enough for both of

you," he said, handing it to Dina first, then wrapping his arms around me again.

"We're actually going to head in," announced Heidi. She stood up, pulling Trey with her. Her lips were closed but it looked like a huge smile was just behind her eyes, about to burst. Trey gave a little wave as they climbed out of the tub.

"Yeah," said Liz. "We should probably go in, too. I feel like a raisin."

Then she turned to Jeremy. "Do you mind letting me back into your room?" she said, blinking slowly.

"Yeah, whatever," said Jeremy. That boy was clueless. Then the two of them got out of the tub and disappeared. Dina mumbled something and left, too.

"I don't know about you, but I could stay here all night," said Drew, turning me around to face him.

"Hmmm?" I said, not because I hadn't heard him but because his nose was so close to mine, and the moon was dipping and rising above his head and the stars were sliding around. I knew I was kind of drunk, but I was pretty sure that it was just the two of us out here in the hot tub, which would mean we were all alone, which would mean . . .

"That is, if you're not too cold?" I followed Drew's

lips as he spoke. They spread out into a wide smile and there were those perfect, square teeth again.

"Cold? Me? No," I slurred. My breath made wild circles of steam in front of my face.

"That's what I'm talking about." He squeezed my arms, and then he ran a hand through my hair. *Keep on breathing, Levy. Wait, who's Levy? Oh, that's me. Right.*

"So, what should we do now?" purred Drew.

I felt my stomach leap into my chest.

"We could play twenty questions again?"

Drew laughed softly. "That's not what I had in mind," he said. He touched my cheek with his hand gently, leading me in, pulling my face forward. This was it. This was really it. The moment I had waited for for fifteen and a half years, spinning right in front of me. I almost said, "I thought you said I was purty." But this wasn't a play. These weren't lines and we weren't Okies. It was really me and this boy — man, actually.

Our lips came together. His lips were warm and soft and tasted like Jack Daniel's and cherry ChapStick. He held my chin and we stayed there for I don't know how long. It was probably thirty seconds or a minute at least. I tried to count but I lost track. And I closed my eyes because I remembered Phoebe and I had talked about that, the importance of eye-closing. But then everything started spinning even faster so I opened them again and Drew was still there, pressed into me. And I didn't want to move, but my nose felt like it was kind of in the way, and I couldn't breathe too well. I hoped he couldn't tell this was my first time really. He pulled back a bit.

"Mmmm," he whispered.

My lips felt tingly out in the open air.

"Pretty nice to have this hot tub all to ourselves, huh?" Drew said. His hand traveled down to the dip between my neck and my collarbone.

"Yeah. Good thing you were prepared." I thought of his bag full of T-shirts and boxers. The bottle of Jack Daniel's. This guy came equipped. "Wait — how did you know we would come out here?"

"I had hopes," he said.

"But —"

And then there was no time for more questions, because his lips were on mine again and he was leaning toward me, his whole body drawing me in. And this time I felt his tongue climbing into my mouth. It was slimy and kind of salty and wiggling around. I knew that I should try to slip my tongue inside his mouth, too. So I pushed and at first it was hard to navigate past his teeth, but then I found space and I tried closing my eyes again and really concentrating. And I was doing it. I, Samantha Iris Levy, was really kissing!

"Mmm, you taste so good," he whispered when we came up for air. "Such kissable lips."

Was I supposed to say thank you? I wasn't sure. Nobody had ever called my lips kissable before. Nobody had ever called them anything before.

"You, too," I mumbled. And then I stopped. Or at least I tried to. The sky was still spinning behind him though.

"Wait!" I managed. And I put a hand on his shoulder. My skin was about five shades paler than his.

"Wait what?" Drew said.

"Nothing. It's just — I can't believe . . ."

I looked at him. It was pretty unbelievable. Yesterday I was whining about Leo Strumm, and now here I was with a Speedo model in a hot tub! How had this happened? I had to call Phoebe and write in my journal and scream from the rooftops. And I didn't want to jump into anything too quickly, but maybe there was such a thing as fate or kismet, and was it okay with him that I had already picked out the colors for our cottage in the backwoods of Burlington and did he want a dog because

I would walk it and feed it and maybe we could get one from the pound, and should we name our firstborn Max or Sebastian, but whatever he wanted really and he would teach skiing during the day and I would make quilts and play the piano and then at night we would lean into each other like this by the fire and tell ghost stories until there were just embers . . . ?

"Whatcha thinking, babe?" His lips were glistening, and now he was kissing the tips of my fingers.

"Me? Nothing."

Yeah. I make out in hot tubs all the time.

"Good. Don't think anymore."

No time for quilts, Levy.

This time, I tried to put my tongue in his mouth first and wiggle it around. I heard him murmur something that sounded like approval, (at least I hoped so. Did I hit a cavity?), and then we were slowly, gently, lying back against the tiled wall of the tub. I felt us sliding down, but I didn't want to say anything.

"Is this okay?" he breathed into my neck.

"Yeah," I whispered back. My tongue felt numb from all the kissing and the whiskey. He ran his hands up the sides of my legs, past my hips, and stopped just below my chest, holding me there.

"Damn, you are just one hot mama."

I started giggling. I couldn't help it. And once I started I couldn't stop.

"What's so funny?"

"Nobody's ever called me a hot mama before."

"Well, they should have, because you are."

He started kissing up my arms to my shoulders and into my neck. *Agh! Just stay away from the ears, please stay away from the ears.* He must have sensed me tensing up, because he came back to my face and found my lips again. And now his hands were moving up, inside my shirt, closing in around my bra.

"I want to do everything with you. I want to explore you," he whispered.

I could feel my breath catch. Everything? What did that mean? Did he want to go all the way? Right here? Right now? I mean, I guess we needed to before we invested in real estate together, but . . . It was all going so fast. I needed to at least make a phone call first. Phoebe!

"What do you think of that?" he said.

"Everything?" I sounded like a squeaking chipmunk.

"Yeah, everything." He traced a finger down my nose. I tried to blink the world into focus, but the sky was still moving so fast behind his head. Then I concentrated on staring just at one of his eyebrows, but it kept moving, too. I wished everything would just stop for a second so I could catch up. I mean, I had imagined this moment for so long. My first time. But I had never pictured it in a hot tub surrounded by towering fir trees in the middle of Nowheresville, Vermont, with a guy who wore goggles and cherry ChapStick, and whom I had just met that day.

"Right here?" I managed to get out.

"Or we could go up to your room," he said, smoothing my hair.

I thought of kids from school — Sara Spencer and Kevin Mallon, Alissa Paulson and Andy Trotts. People were doing it all the time. What was I so scared of? Drew was hotter than both those guys. And older. But . . . but . . .

"But, I mean, I don't know anything about you," I said. I hoped I didn't sound whiny.

Drew laughed softly. "So sweet," he said. "What do you want to know?"

"Um, I don't know. What's your favorite food?" *Nice, Levy. C'mon. You can do better than that.* But Drew just smiled.

"Cheese ravioli with my mom's marinara sauce."

Okay, good answer. He had family values.

"Favorite book?"

"Hmm, I'm more of a magazine guy than books. *Sports Illustrated,* you know, *Maxim,* sometimes *GQ.*"

Okay, well at least he read.

"All right, here's a hard one. Name one reason why I shouldn't like you." To be honest, I hadn't thought of that one by myself. It was from this movie Phoebe and I rented about these kids at summer camp. It was kind of silly I guess, but Drew took it seriously. His eyebrows came together and he bit his lip.

"Hmm. That *is* a hard one. I mean, I think you *should* like me. But if I have to say something then . . . I guess I'm kinda impetuous. Like I see what I want and I go after it. Is that okay?" He came in for another kiss.

"Yeah, that's okay." Better than "I killed a man once" or "I eat babies with duck sauce."

"Do you feel like you know me a little better now?" he asked, grinning.

"I guess . . ."

"Good, because you still haven't answered my question. . . ."

Think, Levy. Think!

"Well, do you want to know more about *me*?" I said, trying to bat my eyelashes like I'd seen Liz do before.

"Sure. Right." He sighed. "Okay, favorite food?"

"Cold pizza! Or really thick bread with butter. The grainy kind. Sometimes garlic potatoes, but they have to be cooked with milk, and I *love* split pea soup. Especially with —"

"Whoa, whoa, whoa!" said Drew.

"Sorry."

"Okay, what else?" he said.

"No, you ask me another," I instructed.

"Right . . . um, favorite book?"

"*Catcher in the Rye*."

"Who's that by?"

I bit my lip. Definite points off.

But not everyone can be a nerd, Levy. Give him a break.

"J. D. Salinger."

"Okay, sorry, never heard of him. And the ten-thousand-dollar question of the night . . . will you sleep with me?" He ducked his face into the water until just his eyes were showing. Did he know I was a sucker for eyes? I tried to smile, but I felt scared and a little bit nauseous. He bobbed up until he was just next to my face, waiting. I had to say *something*.

"I don't know. . . . It's a little cold out here." My voice shook. My tongue felt heavy, but I kept going. "And upstairs . . . um, Jeremy and I are sharing a room, so that might not work." I know you're not supposed to start a long-term relationship by lying, but I was desperate. "Maybe for tonight we could just do some more kissing and stuff first. You know, get to know each other some more . . ."

I was definitely breathing like Darth Vader now, but I couldn't help it. I needed all the air I could get.

"Yeah, I guess so," Drew said slowly. Then he leaned back against the wall next to me and sighed. I looked at the outline of his nose as he gazed up into the trees. His eyes were closed.

Levy! What had I done?

I put my hand on his then tried to sound soft and seductive as I said, "I mean, I had a really good time tonight." He didn't answer.

"I really like kissing you," I said, even lower, touching his shoulder.

"Yeah, I like kissing you, too." His voice was kind of

flat, and his eyes were still closed. Was he going to sleep?

Don't give up, Levy. Just say something. Anything.

"And that was really fun doing karaoke before. Don't you think? Hey! Why didn't you get up and sing?"

"I can't sing," he said.

It was actually true. I had heard him trying to hum along when Stevie D. was up there and Drew was totally off-key, but of course I said, "Of course you can! Anyone can sing! I mean, we can't all be Liz."

"Yeah, Liz looked really hot up there," he said.

I waited for him to continue, but he was quiet. Wasn't he going to say anything about *me* up there?

"Yeah, she did," I added limply.

"Oh, I mean, you looked great up there, too!" He opened his eyes and moved in toward me again. "You were behind Dina most of the time, but I was watching you. You looked really good. And hey —" I felt his arm circling around me again. A shiver ran up my spine. "I had a really good time tonight, too," he whispered, kissing me lightly on the tip of my nose.

Okay, keep the down payment, Levy. Hold off on the dogs. But we're still in the game. I hope.

"Hey, whaddaya say we head back in, huh? It's pretty

frickin' cold out here and I've got to teach again tomorrow, you know."

"Yeah," I said.

"And you, my girl, have a slope to conquer." He picked himself up out of the tub and grabbed a towel from the edge. I followed him out.

"Right." At least he had called me "my girl." That was something, right? Ugh. I didn't feel sure of anything anymore. I was going to be sixteen in a few months, and I had just messed up my one chance to have sex in a hot tub with a guy who had bedroom eyes and skied in the Olympics and loved his mom's ravioli. What was I doing? Why was I such a loser? And now that I was standing upright, the ground was rocking slowly and I had trouble walking in a straight line.

We were by the back door leading into the living room. I could see Dina through the sliding door. She was fast asleep on one of the couches by the fire. Trey and Heidi were nowhere to be found. Neither were Jeremy and Liz. Wonder how *that* turned out. Drew went to open the door, but I pulled at his arm.

"Hey, Drew?"

He turned around.

"Are you, um . . . mad?"

He laughed softly. "Mad? No. Disappointed a little, but not mad."

"You sure?" I asked. Was all hope lost?

"Hey," he touched my cheek. "This is just the beginning, girl. Like you said, we're just getting to know each other. And I'd like to learn a lot more."

He bent down to kiss me. And I leaned into him, feeling his arm wrap around my back. His grip was firm and his lips were warm and full. Yes, I was *his* girl, and he was kissing *me*. Kissing me in front of the stars and the moon and the snow gently clinging to the trees. Kissing *me*, Samantha Levy.

Me and my kissable lips.

Chapter 7

The next morning started with the telephone ringing next to my head. I fumbled before dropping it on the wooden night table.

"Yeah?" my voice was scratchy and slurred. My tongue tasted like a brillo pad.

"Did I wake you, chickadee?" said Dad.

"Nope," I croaked. Dad laughed softly.

"Fun night?" he asked. I heard Kathy murmuring something in the background.

"Uh-huh."

The room slowly started to come into focus. I could see Jeremy's soggy dyspepsia T-shirt hanging over my chair.

"Sounds like it," said Dad. "Honey, Kathy and I are

kinda hungry and I called Jeremy but he's not quite ready yet, either. So we were thinking of heading downstairs. Is that okay?"

"Sure, yeah. That sounds good."

I hung up and fell back onto the pillow. I felt my stomach sloshing around. My head was sloshing around, too. My lips felt raw and chapped from all the cold air and the kissing. I ran my finger across the rough line where they met my skin. Wow. We had done some serious kissing!

I heard Jeremy turn on the shower. I wondered when he got back in with Liz. Had they done it? Was sex all that it was cracked up to be? Mind-changing? Earth-shattering? How did he know to trust this girl Liz whom he had just met and who shook her hips and made kissy faces into the microphone? But he was a boy. It was different for them, right? And then I started picturing them naked and lying on his bed and that was gross because he was my brother, after all.

I slipped on some socks and pulled on my hoodie over my pajamas. Everything felt a little fuzzy and I couldn't move too quickly. Tee-hee! My first real hangover. I was finally a grown-up! Maybe that would mean I had bigger boobs and pouty lips. You know, like in the movies after a crazy party night, when the lead girl looks all disheveled and sultry? I gave a quick look in the mirror. I didn't look too sultry right now. My hair was stuck to the side of my face and there were deep creases from the pillow across my cheeks. Oh, well.

Now I just needed some coffee and to get to the slopes as soon as possible. I stuck my cell phone in my pocket so I could call Phoebe, and then headed downstairs.

The lobby had a strong fire going, and I could hear people in the dining area stirring their coffee and chatting, and the toaster bell announcing fresh English muffins. Everything felt a little too bright and loud. But by far the loudest thing was a woman standing by the front desk, her hands on her hips and her salt-and-pepper nest of hair shaking as she spoke — or rather, yelled. It was the Albert Einstein lady I saw yapping at Phil the first day.

"I expected more out of you! You call this a family business? I could have stayed at a number of different places, but I chose to come here. It is inexcusable!" Her voice was shrill and only added to the throbbing in my head.

"I'm sorry. I really am." Eric was standing behind the desk, speaking slowly, carefully.

"Well, what are you going to do about it is what I want to know? Huh?" the woman screeched.

Eric cleared his throat. "I'll have to talk to my father. We've never really had this situation before. I mean, after we replaced the hot water heater —"

"I'll tell you what you're going to do. You are *obviously* going to have to replace it again! But before you do that, you are going to refund me my money and get on that World Wide Web and you are going to find me another place to stay, mister!" She was shaking a single salmon-colored fingernail in his face.

Who was this lady? Who said "World Wide Web" and called people "mister"?

A lot of people in the dining area had quieted down now and were peering over curiously. Nutbags McScreech just kept right on going.

"Come on! Do it!" she commanded. It was disgusting how she was treating him like he was a disobedient puppy.

"Well, I'd like to refund you, but —" started Eric. I could see he was trying to stay calm, taking deep breaths. But his eyes were blinking furiously.

"Good. Because that's exactly what you're going to do. Do you hear me?" the woman demanded.

"Yes."

"Do you?"

I couldn't take this. I knew it was none of my business, but this was ridiculous. I stepped forward. "Actually, *everyone* can hear you. You're waking up the entire inn." I crossed my arms and tried to exact a menacing gaze.

Lady Einstein spun around like she had been stung by a bee.

"And who are *you*?" She looked me slowly up and down, her lips pressed together in disgust.

"Sam Levy." I almost said, "The one with the kissable lips," but I refrained. "And I *was* going to have a cup of coffee and sit by the fire, but you kind of ruined that plan."

"Well, excuuuuuuse me," she sneered. "Do you know what ruined my morning?"

"No. What?"

"When I went to get into my shower, there was no hot water. No! Hot! Water!"

"Well, I'm sorry, but that's no reason to —"

"And this young man says he doesn't know what he can do about it. I mean, really!"

"I'm sorry, and *how* is this his fault?" I asked, hands on hips.

She puffed out her cheeks and spluttered. Her lips were colored the same salmon as her nails, and they were thin and flaky. She should learn about cherry ChapStick.

"Well, he *works* here, doesn't he?"

"It's a very old building," started Eric.

"I'm not talking to you right now. You had your chance."

I was seriously going to kick this lady in the teeth.

"No, you had *your* chance. It's not his fault that there was no hot water. Maybe it's because you used it up taking a bubble bath the night before. I don't know. And I don't care! All I know is that is no way to treat somebody who has opened up his home to you. So you think about how to speak to someone before you open your mouth again, because if I were him, I wouldn't give you any refund. I would tell you to pack your bags and get out of here!"

I hadn't meant to go that far. But once again, my mouth was moving faster than my brain, and by the time I stopped, I was breathless. Both Einstein and Eric were staring at me, wide-eyed and stunned.

Finally, Eric spoke. "Mrs. Briley —" he began.

"No, that's okay," she said. Her voice was a lot lower

and softer now. "I'll be speaking to your father as soon as he comes in. Make sure you tell him it is *urgent*. And you —" She turned back to me, her teeth gritted together. "You have quite a mouth on you, young lady. You'd better watch it or one day it is going to get you into some serious, I mean *serious* trouble." Her nostrils flared but I just concentrated on her flaky lips and didn't budge an inch. Then she grabbed an apple from the front desk and marched up the stairs and down the hall.

As soon as we heard her door slam, I burst into giggles. Eric was laughing, too.

"What a witch," I said.

"Yeah," he said.

"Sorry I went off like that. Sometimes I get a little carried away. And she just pushed all my buttons."

"No, I loved it. My dad always says to let him handle anyone who's trouble, but I was having a really hard time."

"Yeah, well . . ."

I nodded. My head felt heavy. I really needed some coffee. And there was something really unnerving about just standing in front of this guy. I thought of him sitting in the dark, drawing. He was kind of weird.

Dad and Kathy were in the corner by one of the floor-to-ceiling windows. "What was that all about?" Dad asked when I came over.

"Oh, nothing. Never mind," I said, grabbing a coffee cup.

"Wanna join us for breakfast?"

He and Kathy both had plates full of eggs and bacon. I was pleasantly surprised to see Kathy chewing away. I had pegged her as a strictly cantaloupe girl. But still, the thought of food and Kathy made me pretty queasy right now.

"Sorry, gotta make a phone call," I said, and headed out of the dining room.

I plopped down at my usual spot in front of the fire. I was thinking about getting a sign for this chair that said: Back off. Levy territory.

Mmm, the coffee felt good.

"'lo?" Her voice was faint and sleepy.

"Pheebs!"

"Hey, Sam!"

"Did I wake you?"

"No." I knew she was lying and that I should let her go back to sleep. But I couldn't help myself.

"Oh, Pheebs, it was amazing! We sang 'Lost and

Found' — just the girls — and I closed my eyes like you said. And then we all went into this hot tub — did you get that? Hot tub? And Drew and I kissed — a *lot*. And it was *really* fun kissing him and did I mention he has this blond spiky hair and these incredible eyes and he almost went to the Olympics and he reads ravioli and eats lots of magazines but — no, wait. Whatever. You know what I mean. We actually didn't do much talking; mostly kissing, but he told me I have kissable lips. Can you believe that? Is that even a real adjective? Kissable?"

"I think —"

"But I didn't let him see my ears, even though he was really close and then he said, 'I want to *explore* you' and I was, like, what? And he totally wanted to have sex! And of course I freaked out and told him that I couldn't because I was sharing a room with Jeremy, just because, I don't know. I mean, I just met him, like, twenty-four hours ago, but I mean, no it's been forty-eight, but still I don't know, I don't even know if he's a serial killer or if he has a middle name or works for the CIA or anything! Help!"

"Okay, first of all Sam, that's *fantastic*. And, do you realize how fantastic this is?"

"Oh! And you know what the best thing about him

is? He is nothing like Leo! I've totally moved on. I am over him. You were so right, Pheebs. I just needed some crisp mountain air and a few kisses in a hot tub to realize there are other fish in the sea, you know? I mean, what did Leo and I have in common really except the play, right? We never really *talked*. I think I idealized him because he was my first kiss, but it wasn't really a kiss. I mean, who says 'purty' right? And now that I've really been kissed, it's so completely different. I mean, Drew is more confident, more serious, more mature. . . .

"I wish that you could meet him, Pheebs. Well, maybe you will. Maybe he'll come down to New York for spring break. I bet he has frequent flyer miles. Did I mention he's *eighteen*! Oh! it looks like my dad and Kathy are done with breakfast. I gotta get ready to go to the slopes. Hey, but wait — I didn't hear anything about you."

"Oh, nothing. Same old. You're the one with news." Phoebe sounded excited for me, but there was definitely a little edge in her voice. Uh-oh.

"How's Grandma?" I asked.

"Okay, I guess. She called me Florence the whole time, and she can't find her cockatoo."

"And what'd you do last night?"

"Murphy's. The usual crowd."

"Any time with Paprika?"

"No, but I didn't even see him."

"Really? Why not?"

"Oh . . . I don't know . . . It just wound up being a few of us watching movies. It was stupid." She sounded distracted and there was this weird pause at the end of her sentence. But then, before I could cut in, she started again, cheery and bright. "Anyway, you gotta go. You've got a *man* waiting for you."

"Yeah!" I said. I tried to sound upbeat, too.

"Call me later," she said.

"Or you call me!" But she had already clicked OFF.

Chapter 8

By the time we got to Sugar Peak, there was already a long line for the ski rentals. It was so hot in the chalet with all the furry collars and matching leg warmers. Dad and Kathy were going back out to some of the cross-country trails, and Jeremy and I got fitted and headed to the chairlift. I tried not to look too eager as I searched for Drew's dirty-blond spikes and orange goggles. It was 10:30. He would be teaching his new class by now, right?

"Looking for someone?" I felt a hand on my shoulder. I gasped, turning around.

"Gotcha!" said Jeremy, his eyes on fire, his freckles laughing.

"Dumb butt," I said, and punched him in the arm.

"Oh, come on. Can't you take a joke?"

"Not funny," I replied, pushing past him. The chairlift came, and we slid into our seats.

"Come on, Sam. You can't take everything so seriously. Anyway, how was it?"

"Fine." There was no way I was talking about this with Jeremy. "So, what's up with you and Liz?"

"Oh, you know. Whatever," he said.

"What's that? Whatever. You left the hot tub together."

"Sam, it's none of your business."

"Jeremy has a new girlfriend," I sang. I know. I definitely regress about ten years when I'm around him sometimes.

"No I *don't,*" he said, annoyed.

"But why not? She seems pretty cool and she was really into you — which, let me tell you, Jer — it takes a special breed of woman to want to be with you. It probably takes —"

"Listen, Sam. Just shut up, okay? I didn't want to do anything with her because I — whatever. I just wasn't interested." And now his voice was more than annoyed. It was teetering on real anger.

"*Okay,* I get it," I said.

"Listen," he said, softer this time. "Just, don't go blabbing about this to any of your friends like Phoebe or . . . *Rachel,* okay?" He looked me right in the eye. And I knew he was waiting for me to answer.

"Fine," I said, rolling my eyes.

"Promise?" he pushed.

"Yes, okay! Jeesh!" Wow, that was really good ammunition. Rachel was friends with this girl from the orchestra named Anna. I knew that Jeremy and she had hooked up once at a party. Rachel had told me. But when I asked him about it he, of course, wouldn't tell me anything. I didn't know that he was still interested. I have to say, even though I acted like he was bugging me, I was kind of impressed. Maybe Jeremy wasn't such an unfeeling robot after all.

It didn't take long for him to break my little reverie, though.

"Besides, Sam, we're only here for a week. It's stupid to get involved with someone."

"Right," I said.

"You know that, don't you?" he asked.

"Yeah, whatever."

"Sam, I'm talking about *you*."

"What? Who said I was getting *involved*?"

"It's all over your face."

"No it's not."

"Yes it is."

"Not it's not!"

Ugh. How did he always turn it back to me? "Whatever," he said. "Remember, we came here for Dad and to ski."

"Right." My stomach felt even more twisted than before. Because I guess part of me thought Jeremy had a good point. I mean, we *were* only here for a week. What did I expect, anyway? To meet the man of my dreams? To fall in love? And was Drew really the one? He said things like, "That's what I'm talking about," and "hot mama." And he didn't read books. Not that I was in any position to judge. Before last night, the most action I had gotten was from a down pillow. I thought of Drew's lips tracing a path down my neck. I felt my breath get quick and shallow. And I was glad we hadn't gone any further last night.

We pushed off the chair at the top. I had forgotten what a thrill it was to jump off. Jeremy was totally unimpressed that I came to a perfect T-stop, but I didn't need his opinion any more this morning. There were colorful jackets and pom-pom hats zipping down the sides of the mountain in every direction. No sign of Drew, though. Where was that area that he took us to yesterday?

"Hey, so I was gonna check out the Pine Bluffs trail today. Aaron says it's got some cool inclines," said Jeremy.

Might as well, Levy. It beat going back to the Junior Slope alone. Where was the Junior Slope anyway? I could picture myself foraging for nuts and berries in the woods after taking a wrong turn.

Pine Bluffs looked really challenging. Lots of turns and twists, even some little jumps. I tried to remember what Drew had taught me about leaning into one leg and then another. I tried to think about how he had me bend my knees and stay low to the ground. But I have to admit, I was mostly thinking about his hands on my waist. And then on my neck and in my hair.

"This look okay to you?" asked Jeremy.

"Uh-huh," I said, but I was still thinking about those hands.

"Okay, then. See you at the bottom, nerd," said Jeremy, and he pushed off, snaking his way along the path.

I looked around me. We were pretty high up. Above the tree line. The air felt thin and sharp. C'mon Levy.

You can do this. You're strong. Lean into it. Concentrate. Leave the behind — agh! That was too ridiculous.

I did pretty well. Got about a third of the way down before I fell, but I knew how to brace myself. The rest of the way, it was a series of short runs and some scooting on my butt.

Jeremy was waiting for me at the bottom of the trail.

"And, bringing up the *rear* for the Turtle team, is Samantha Levy!"

"Thank you! Thank you very much!" I said in my best Elvis impersonation.

"Again?" Jeremy asked.

"Sure."

We did Pine Bluffs another three more times before Jeremy decided he was hungry and we should go to the chalet for some lunch.

Lunch. I felt sick and excited at the same time. Drew would be taking his lunch break, too, now, right?

The chalet was packed again, of course. And now there was the smell of hamburgers and pizza. Mmmm. Even with a nervous stomach, I had worked up an appetite. Jeremy waved me over to his place in line, but I was busy looking for something else. If only some of these fluffy coats would move.

I saw his blond hair first. He was over at the table by the hot chocolate bar, sitting with what I guessed was his class from that morning — a middle-aged couple, a man with gray hair and glasses, and two girls and a guy about my age. One of the girls was wearing a lavender turtleneck sweater and had long, honey-colored braids. She was leaning across the table and was talking with her hands, and Drew was tipping his head back and laughing.

My heart jumped. Was I supposed to play it cool and just eat with Jeremy and see if Drew noticed me? Or did I need to say something? Maybe just walk over there and say something casual like:

Hey, last night was really special and I think you're a great kisser and I don't want you to think that just because I was too freaked out to have sex that I'm not interested because I am very interested and as a matter of fact maybe I am ready to have sex but I just have to talk to my friend Phoebe some more or maybe I should call my mom but she might be with Jon who has a gross ponytail. So I guess, yeah, let's just do it, right? But maybe we could talk before, during, and afterward so I'm not so scared. Oh, and hey, you want one of my French fries?

Yeah, that would do the trick, Levy.

We paid for our food, and then Jeremy spotted Dad

and Kathy at a table all the way in the back of the room by the bathrooms. I groaned.

"Come on. Play nice," Jeremy instructed. We made our way over and sat down.

"How was it, you two?" gushed Kathy.

"Oh, great," said Jeremy. "What about you?"

"Really nice," said Dad.

"Beautiful! Magnificent! Fantabulous!" Kathy exclaimed.

Ugh. I wanted to tell her I was allergic to adjectives. I really had decided in the car that morning that I was going to try and ignore her. But she sure was making it hard.

"Did you love it? Was it awesome?" she continued. This lady just didn't give up.

"Yeah, it was fun," said Jeremy. Then he turned to me and mouthed, "Nice."

"Yeah, fun," I echoed, biting into my sandwich.

That was all Kathy needed.

"Yay! Where'd you go? What'd you see?" she chirped. I'd let Jeremy handle that one. I had work to do. The three of them started chatting away about the tremendous sights and breathtaking heights while I shoved my fries into my mouth and scanned the crowd for Drew's blond hair.

There he was. Still with Honey Braids in the lavender. *Breathe and chew, Levy.*

Breathe and chew.

But it was pointless. I soon got the hiccups from inhaling my food too fast.

"Oh, Sam. Come on. Just go over and say something already." Jeremy's mouth was, of course, full of American cheese.

"Go over where?" asked Kathy.

None of your business, I thought. But I just pretended not to hear and punched Jeremy in the leg.

"You're a wimp," he muttered.

Time to prove him wrong.

I took a slow sip of Diet Coke and stood up.

"Okay, I'll be right back," I announced.

"Where is she going?" I heard Dad say. But I didn't wait to hear Jeremy's answer. I was on a mission. I could do this.

Most of the group had finished their meals and were just watching Honey Braids. She was still talking, her hands waving wildly in the air.

"And all of a sudden, this bear was in our tent. And we were like, aaaaaaaaaah!" she recounted with a syrupy Southern twang.

"Whoa!" said Drew, leaning back in his chair.

I stepped up to the edge of the table. "Um, Drew?"

"Yeah? Oh, hey, Sam!" Was he excited to see me? I couldn't tell.

"Hey. I just wanted to say . . . *hep!*"

"What?"

"Sorry, I have the hiccups. *Hep!* I just wanted to say . . . hey."

"Hey," he said again. He gave me a slight smile, but didn't say anything else.

I obviously hadn't thought this through too far. Was that it?

Quick! Think, Levy, think. Use the noggin.

I sucked in my breath. "Jeremy and I did the Pine Bluffs trail this morning. *Hep!*"

"Really? How did that go?" He nodded his head like he was impressed. At least, that's what I hoped it meant.

"Good! I mean, really awesome. *Hep!*"

"That's what I'm talking about." He gave me a high five. Not exactly romantic, but at least it was physical contact, right?

"Hey listen, Sam. I'm glad you found us. I have to get back to class, but a bunch of us were going to go to the

Fondue Pot tonight. This place in town. If you want to come, they have these big pots in the middle of the table with cheese and chocolate. It's crazy good. And they have a special on hot toddies Tuesday nights."

"Mmmm," said Honey Braids, patting her stomach.

"What do you think?" Drew's eyes narrowed on me now, and his voice was quiet and close, like it was just for us to hear.

"Sure!" I said, maybe a little too fast. "*Hep!*"

"Sweet. I'll pick you up at the inn around 6:30. And bring your brother, too, if you want." He winked at me and turned back to the table. "All right, folks. Who's staying with me for the afternoon? Let's hit it."

Wait. Was I just invited out on a date with my brother? And was Honey Braids coming, too? But I couldn't think about that now. I had to think positive and remember the way Drew's eyes looked like dazzling blue marbles and his lips came together, smooth and shiny and the way that — *hep!* Ugh. Still had those hiccups.

I made my way back to our lunch table in the back.

"Hey, guess who found us," Jeremy said, barely moving his lips. Liz was standing next to him in her white furry jacket. She had a new, long scarf in pink and red, and her cheeks were the same colors, warm and rosy.

"Heard you did PB!" she said.

"Huh?"

"Pine Bluffs," explained Jeremy.

"Oh, yeah," I said.

"Wow! Would you be up for doing it again with me this afternoon? Heidi and Dina were lame-o's and stayed back at our hotel." She looked from me to Jeremy, so hopeful. I felt a little bad for her. I knew what it was like to want to be liked.

"Sure," I said, and hooked my arm through hers.

Chapter 9

No answer.

I speed-dialed again. Straight to voice mail.

Where could she be? I needed to check in with Phoebe before Drew picked me up. I was outside on the front steps of the inn, stamping my feet to keep warm. Under my jacket all I had on was a clingy black cardigan and jeans. I know, yawn. But it was the only thing I could come up with. I also blow-dried my hair upside down and did the electric socket dance. That's when I run around shaking my head and arms as fast as I can like I've just been electrocuted. It's the only way I know how to get my hair to look like it has some body to it. It never stays bouncy for very long, but it's still fun to dance around in my underwear.

And now I really needed some Phoebe advice. What if Drew had gone home and decided he didn't want to kiss geeks with long ears anymore? Honey Braids had looked much hipper than me. Or what if he *did* still want to kiss me, and do everything else, too?

I speed-dialed Phoebe again. Nothing.

I heard the front door open behind me and then a dog raced across the front lawn. I love dogs. We used to have a mutt named Simon when I was little — part terrier, part golden retriever. This one was black and tan and looked like it was some sort of mix, but I couldn't tell, maybe Labrador, maybe husky. Anyway, he was really beautiful. And fast.

"Hey," came a voice behind me. It was what's-his-face — Eric.

"Hey."

"How did skiing go today?" he asked.

"Good. We did the Pine Bluffs trail," I said.

"Nice! That's tricky."

"Yeah."

Eric threw a stick out into the snow. We both watched as the dog tore across the lawn to retrieve it, then brought it back to Eric's feet. He threw it out again.

"Hey, listen. I just wanted to say thank you for sticking up for me this morning in front of that lady."

"Sure, whatever." I was thinking of reminding him that *he* was the one who lectured me about my temper just a few days ago, but I let it go. New Year's Resolution: no more grudges. Except for Kathy. Okay, fewer grudges. I had a few more days before New Year's Eve. Agh! Would I still be a virgin next year?

"So, are you, um . . . going out?" Eric asked.

"Yeah," I bit my lip to keep from smiling too goofily. "Any minute now, actually."

"With your friends from last night?"

"Yeah, some of them."

"Drew?" Wait, how did he know Drew?

"As a matter of fact, yes."

"Sounds like fun. Hot Toddy Tuesdays?"

"Yesss," I said slowly. What was this, twenty questions — the *un*fun edition?

"Listen, Sam. This is none of my business, and I shouldn't be butting in but — well, I don't want you to take this the wrong way. But Drew is kind of . . . well, he goes out with a lot of the vacationers, and uh . . ."

He kicked at a small chunk of ice on the walk.

"What are you saying?" I said. My mouth felt dry and thick.

"Well, I mean, it's none of my business —"

"Yeah, you said that already." Now I was getting angry.

"But I've just seen him . . . oh, never mind."

What was *with* this guy? Who did he think he was? And what did he know about Drew? He had no idea what Drew was like! I'd bet Eric had never even slept with someone. What a jerk! And then I thought about Drew that afternoon with Honey Braids. I remembered her patting her belly. *Mmmm.* I wasn't about to tell Eric that she was probably coming out tonight, too. Whatever. She was just one of his students, right? I wasn't about to get jealous after one night of kissing. We weren't even dating yet, were we? Agh! For the second time, this strange guy had rendered me completely speechless, and I was *pissed.*

"Well, yeah, that's it." He whistled and the dog came bounding over. "I just wanted to warn you because . . . I don't know, you were really nice to me this morning and . . ." He puffed out his cheeks. "Now I feel like an ass."

"Oh, really? Well, that's probably because you just *acted* like an ass," I said. His forehead pulled into a frown. But I kept going. "Listen, I'm kinda sick of your little lessons on family values and dating. I'm not about to marry this guy, I'm just going out to have hot toddies and fondue and I don't need you to tell me whether that's a good idea or not! And if you think —"

"Sam?"

Drew! I turned around. His blond hair was rumpled and his cheeks were windburned. I wanted to run into his arms and have him scoop me up into the air. But then again, knowing me, I'd probably knock us both over.

"Eric, right?" said Drew.

"Yeah. Hey," said Eric, throwing the stick out again.

"Did I . . . interrupt something?" Drew asked carefully.

Oh, no. How had he gotten here? How much had he heard? I looked around to see if I could find his car. He must have come around back from the parking lot. But I didn't care. I just wanted to leave now.

"No! Not at all! Let's go!" And I grabbed his hand. It was big and warm.

"That guy lives there, right?" Drew asked as we got into his black Jetta. The heat went on full blast and I wanted so badly to just have the hot air blow away all the clouds that were fogging up my head.

"Yeah, I guess." I said.

"Was he bugging you?" Drew asked.

"No. Did you hear — ?"

Drew shook his head before I could finish. "I was too busy staring at your hair."

Yay, electric socket dance! "It's usually really flat. But I have this trick," I started. But Drew cut me off again, this time with his lips. I could smell his cherry ChapStick, could feel his cold nose on my skin. And it felt great. I closed my eyes and tried to shut out the past ten minutes with Eric. What did he know anyway? And who cared what Drew had done in the past? Or how many girls he had dated? He was with *me* now.

By the time we got to the Fondue Pot, there was already a table set up in the back for us. I recognized some of the people from his lunchtime crowd. Honey Braids was there, still in her lavender sweater.

"Hey, y'all!" she called when she saw us.

I squeezed Drew's hand and gave her a huge smile as we sat down.

There were a couple of other people from their class,

too. I saw two of the girls look at my hand in Drew's and then lean in to each other and whisper something. It felt good. Liz and Dina were there, too. Liz looked really disappointed when she saw that Jeremy wasn't with me.

"He has a bad cold, I think from being out in the hot tub," I told her. I didn't want to lie, but I thought it was nicer than saying he and Aaron were watching wrestling matches on pay-per-view.

The waitress came around and everybody dug into their pockets and bags. I took a deep breath. It was the first time that I was using my fake ID. Phoebe and Rachel and I had gotten them as a dare last year when we turned fifteen. My name was Anne Susan Spencer, which made me laugh because my initials spelled "ass." I never used it because we never went to bars, anyway. But it was fun to pull it out of my wallet. I saw Drew look at me and grin. We all ordered hot toddies; Drew explained that they were whiskey with honey and lemon. Yeesh. More whiskey. I knew I had to take it slower with the drinking tonight. Then we decided on one cheese pot and one chocolate pot for the table. Everybody started talking about the snow and which trails were the best to go on.

Honey Braids turned to me and said, "Hey, I'm

Ashley." She had warm brown eyes and a mess of freckles on her nose and cheeks.

"I'm Sam."

"Yeah, I know. I'm really glad you decided to come. Drew was talking about how much fun you are!"

I felt a smile sneak across my lips.

"Really?"

See? What did Eric know? I wasn't just some girl. I watched Drew as he talked with some of his students. They were asking him about the Olympics. Of course, I had heard it before, but I loved to listen to his voice and have an excuse to just gaze at him.

Then our drinks came. Liz stood up and tapped on one of the water glasses.

"Excuse me! Excuse me! I would like to make a toast. To an awesome week in Vermont. To making new friends. And to Drew for teaching us to tackle the slopes and to leave your behind — *behind*!" Good for her. Conquer the cheese factor. Everybody laughed and tipped their glasses back. The drink was lemony and sweet. Then I felt Drew's hand inch across my thigh and give me a gentle squeeze. Oops. I forgot to swallow and instead sputtered and coughed.

Smooth, Levy, real smooth.

Drew laughed quietly and patted me on the back. "Easy, rock star," he whispered.

I definitely needed to loosen up. I picked up my glass and took another big gulp. So much for taking it slow. Tonight was going to be all about having fun.

Chapter 10

❄❄❄❄❄❄❄❄❄❄❄❄❄❄❄❄❄❄❄

"You taste like chocolate and cheese and marshmallows," I murmured, giggling.

Drew and I were parked somewhere between the Fondue Pot and the inn. He had turned off the headlights and made the front car seats lean all the way back. The sky was dancing around again from the two and a half hot toddies I'd had. The stars looked like they were being swallowed up by the inky night.

"Don't forget the bread and apples. Mmm, I could kiss you all night," he said, leaning in again.

His hands were big and strong, and he was running them through my hair, up along my neck, and — eek! — really close to my ears! I guided his hands back down to my shoulders. He didn't seem to notice. Just kept kissing me, down one cheek and across my chin. And then he was unzipping my jacket and moving his hands up under my sweater. I was kind of ticklish and definitely nervous, but I tried not to flinch.

Stay calm, Levy. Stay calm. This is what normal people do. Sara Spencer and Kevin Mallon are probably doing it right now. Pretend this is health class. It's natural.

I felt the cold air hit my bare stomach. I couldn't take it.

"Hey, Drew?" I said timidly.

"Don't worry, Sammy," he whispered. "I have a condom." His lips were inching down to my chest. His fingers were on my top jeans button. I moved my hands and held his firmly. Then I took in a deep breath and summoned up my fifteen and a half years of virginal courage.

"Drew? I don't think I can do this right now." My words tumbled out and it felt like my teeth were too big for my mouth.

He stopped. "I thought you were having fun," he said.

"I was. I am. I just — I'm not quite ready to do all that, you know. Right now. I'm . . . I'm . . ."

Drew fell back in his seat and blew out a long sigh.

"Wow," he said. His face was hidden in shadow. But that was okay — I didn't think I could look at it anyway.

"I mean, I still want to kiss you and do all that other stuff, I just don't know if I'm ready for sex right now. Is all."

He was still just lying there, looking at the ceiling of the car. Everything was incredibly still now. Too still. I waited, but, of course, my mind was racing. Pretty soon more thoughts came spilling out.

"I mean, I'm really having fun. I just thought, maybe we could get to know each other first. I mean, I know you, but I don't really *know* you, you know? Like, I know you ski and you like reading *Sports Illustrated*, which is cool, but do you do other things, like play an instrument or go camping, or . . . I don't know. Are you allergic to anything I should know about?"

It was meant to be a joke, sort of, but it wasn't funny. I kept going.

"Like, here's a couple of things you might not know about me. I do the school newspaper and last year I was in this play, but whatever. My friends Phoebe and Rachel and I volunteer sometimes at this nursing home and I mean it's kinda boring but they're really sweet and this one guy named Mr. Keys thinks he's still a general in the army and he calls us to attention — it's pretty funny, but I mean, when I get that old I'm sure I'll be wandering around in a shower cap getting lost in the frozen food section of the grocery store, or I think I may move to Utah. But blah, blah, blah. Tell me about you! What are you thinking? And what do you like? And yeah, what are you thinking? Let's just *talk* some more."

"Sam, didn't we do this last night?" Drew's voice sounded tired.

"Yeah, but I mean, you said that was just the beginning, remember?"

"Sure," he said, but he still wouldn't look at me. He just sighed again. "You do a lot of *talking,* Sam. Like too much sometimes. Sometimes you gotta let your body take over instead of your mind."

Maybe he was right. After all, he had been at this longer than I had. But I knew I wasn't ready for sex. Not in a steamy Jetta. Not — no, not at all. Not now.

I tried again, softer this time. "It's just, there's so much to learn about each other. Like, tell me about the Olympics!"

"I've never been."

"Yeah, but, the trials. I mean, are you gonna try out again?"

"I guess."

"Cool!" Another silence. Ugh. "Hey, Drew?"

"Yeah?"

"There are other things besides sex that we could do." I tried to snuggle down next to him. But now it felt like I didn't fit there. Like I had too many limbs or something. "Do you wanna . . . ?" I started kissing him up under his chin. He had a small scar running just under his jaw, and I touched my lips to it as tenderly as I could.

"Hey, Sam?"

"Yeah?" I whispered.

"Sorry, I'm just not feeling it so much right now, you know? Wind's kinda sucked outta my sails," he said.

"Yeah, okay," I said, deflating steadily.

And then we just lay there. I pulled down my sweater because I felt stupid lying there with my stomach in the moonlight.

"Listen, I think maybe I should just take you back to the inn, okay?" Drew said.

"Sure," I heard myself say. But I didn't feel connected to it. I didn't feel connected to anything anymore.

We drove the rest of the way in silence. I really didn't want to cry. *Please, Levy. Hold it together until we get back.* I hoped Phoebe had her phone with her now, wherever she was. When we got to the inn, Drew pulled up outside the front, and kept the car idling.

"I had a really good time tonight," I managed to say. "Did you?"

"Yeah."

"I mean, I hope we can do more of what we were doing and stuff. And maybe pretty soon we can do more. I just want to get to know you more before —"

"Yeah, I get it," he said, still looking forward.

"Is that okay?"

"Yeah, sure." But he wasn't leaning in to give me a kiss, or stroke my hair, or anything.

"Really?"

"Yeah." Finally, he turned to face me, but his eyes looked cold and small now.

"Well, I guess I'll see you tomorrow then?" I said with what I hoped was a smile.

He gave a short nod.

I leaned in and kissed him lightly on the lips. Then I opened the car door. I wanted so badly for him to say "Stop!" or grab my arm and pull me into him, but he didn't. He didn't do anything. And I walked back into the inn, the world still feeling wobbly beneath my feet, but now for an entirely different reason.

Chapter 11

There was definitely something going on. I had tried Phoebe about a hundred times when I got back to the inn last night and then again this morning. Still no answer. I hoped it wasn't something bad with her grandma. She had been sick for a while. But Phoebe would've called me if something happened, right? Was there something she wasn't telling me?

Finally, I gave up and headed out to Sugar Peak with Dad, Kathy, and Jeremy. I was not in great shape. My lips were puffy and my head was pounding and there seemed to be a lot more turns in the drive over. But this wasn't just a hangover. This was something much heavier weighing me down.

Jeremy announced he was going to take a snowboarding class. Dad asked if I wanted to join them for cross-country, but I said no, even though I wasn't sure who I was going to hang out with. I seriously considered parking myself in front of the fire, but somehow it felt too sad without Margie and her interactive sweater. I strapped myself into my giant-sized boots and then got in line for the chairlift — alone.

I saw Liz and Dina and Heidi sometime later in the morning. I had just done an advanced beginner slope called Mystic Mountain or Magic Mists. Something like that. It was pretty fun, I guess. I spent a fair portion of the trip down on my butt, of course.

I recognized Liz's furry hood first.

"Hey!" I called.

Dina turned around and smiled. "Oh, hey, Sam!"

"Sammy!" said Heidi with a big wave. Liz was busy fixing something on her skis.

"Missed you guys last night," I said when I got close enough to actually talk instead of shout.

"Yeah, I was having fun being lazy and Miss Heidi here was busy with Nate." Dina nudged Heidi in the ribs. But she didn't have to. Heidi's smile was already so big it took up her whole face.

"I thought his name was Trey."

Heidi scrunched up her nose.

"No. Different guy," she said. "Nate's a *bartender*."

"Okay, okay. We all know that Heidi's gotten a lot of action. Let's just get back to the lift, okay? Some of us are trying to do some skiing, you know," said Liz.

"Liz thinks she saw this cute guy from our first class out here," Dina said out of the side of her mouth. "Manhunt," she added in a whisper. But Liz saw the whole thing.

"Listen, little Miss I-already-have-someone-I'm-so-perfect-and-cute-and-happy, just because you like to stay at home and paint your nails and talk to lover-boy on the phone, doesn't mean that I have to sit home and watch you." Her voice was nasal and she looked like she was biting off her words. Then she turned to me for the first time.

"How's your brother, Sam?" she said with a sneer.

"Fine, I guess."

"Well, I think he's an ass."

I started laughing. I couldn't help it. It was just that I had never heard someone else call him that besides me. But Liz didn't find it funny at all.

"Whatever. We gotta go. You guys ready?"

Dina rolled her eyes and Heidi mouthed "Sorry" and then the three of them were off.

Wow. Now I *really* missed Phoebe.

I spent most of lunch in the bathroom, avoiding Drew. He was over at a table full of people. Lots of girls, of course. I knew I wanted to say something to him, like about the importance of connecting with people before you have sex, and how I thought we really "got" each other. But would he care?

My pocket was vibrating. I pulled out my phone.

The caller ID said PHEEBS. Finally!

"Hey!"

"Sam!"

"Where have you been? Are you okay? Is it Grandma? What's going on?!"

"I . . . miff . . . er."

We were breaking up.

"I'll call you right back!" I shouted, then threw open the stall door. A woman at the mirror stared at me angrily. "This is supposed to be —"

"Sorry!" I yelped, running out the door. The chalet was way too loud. I tried to find a closet or a hidden corner. Nothing. Forget it. I raced outside and dialed her number again. Yipes! It was cold without a coat on.

"'lo?"

"Pheebs?"

"Hey, Sam. How's it going?"

"Fine! Well, not fine. But more on that later. How are *you*?"

"Good."

"You sure?"

"Yeah." She sounded really far away, though. And then there was a long pause. "Listen, Sam, can I — can we maybe talk later? I guess I wanted to talk to you, but . . . pickle."

Pickle was our code word for *somebody just walked in the room who I can't talk in front of.* It was usually one of our parents or something. It was kind of not very subtle to say "pickle" in the middle of a sentence, but — oh, well.

"Yeah, sure Pheebs. I'll call you tonight. Okay? Or you call me."

"Yeah, let's talk tonight."

"But you're sure you're okay?"

"Yeah," she said quickly, then "Bye!" and hung up. What was *that*? I spent a few minutes just looking at the phone, wishing she would call back and explain. She'd never acted like this before. By the time I got back into the chalet, it was clearing out. I guessed I had missed my opportunity to talk to Drew at lunch. But he could've found me to talk to if he wanted. Something told me he didn't want to, though. My stomach hurt thinking about it.

"There you are!" said Dad, coming over with Kathy. "You disappeared on us at lunch."

"Yeah, sorry."

"Kathy saved you this turkey sandwich, if you want it," Dad said, as Kathy reached out and handed me a bundle in a paper napkin and then smiled shyly.

"It's pretty yummy," she said.

"Thanks," I said coldly. Ugh. She just wanted me to like her. Why couldn't Drew try this hard?

"So, meet you back here, usual time?" said Dad.

"Sure," I said.

I decided to go back to Pine Bluffs again. I actually managed to get through almost the whole trail on my feet on the first try. It felt pretty good, too. But, of course, there was nobody to share my success with. I made my way back to the lift.

"Hey, partner!" I heard behind me. It was that girl Ashley with the braids, from the night before. "How's it going?" She gave me a hug like we were best buddies. It was a little odd, considering how Liz had treated me that morning and how funky my real best friend had just acted.

"I'm okay," I lied. "How are you?"

"Great! Wasn't that fun last night? Seemed like you and Drew were having a total blast." Ugh. I guess there were *two* people who still said "total blast."

"Sort of." I moved forward so she would know that I didn't feel like talking about it. But she slid in right next to me.

"Hey, I won't pry. Just wanted to see if you wanted to go up together?"

"Sure." Why not, right?

The whole way up the mountain, Ashley talked about how she'd never seen so much snow in her life. She was from a farm in Texas and the only time she had seen snow was in one of those globes that her mom brought back from a trip to Minnesota where you could turn it upside down and then watch the city sparkle with glittery flakes. She was in West Lake with her best friend, Emily, so they could learn how to ski. But Emily had woken up with a fever and chills that morning.

"Poor darlin'. I left her surrounded by a sea of tissues.

Not much of a vacay, huh?" Ashley loved to abbreviate random words like that. Like I soon learned that "tote hilare" meant "totally hilarious" — one of her favorite phrases. As in "Did you see that dude in the spandex pants and the matching vest?! That was tote hilare!" Or "They serve Jell-O without cool whip on top! Isn't that just tote hilare?!" Somehow with her southern lilt it worked. And she was the first person I'd ever met who could talk faster than me. It was fun to hear her chirp and tweet about the snow, the air, the beauty of it all.

When we got to the top of the lift and landed, she glided over to a ledge a little farther than I'd been before. Then she opened her arms and tilted her face up into the sun. "I just love it!" she sang. Her braids fell down her back, her lips smiling up into the sky. "C'mere, look at this!" she said.

I was going to tell her that I had a lot on my mind right now and maybe I would later, but she didn't even wait for my response. "Come *here*!" She pulled me over to where she was standing. The whole city of West Lake lay below. And beyond that, miles and miles of mountains and plains.

"Wow," I heard myself say.

"Yeah. Pretty phenom, huh?" she said. "Hard to find

too many things wrong with the world when you see it from up here."

She was right. Maybe I was taking myself a little too seriously. Nobody had died or anything. Phoebe was acting a little strange. I'd hear the whole story later. And I just needed to talk to Drew so we could get on the same page, too. I didn't need this whole sex thing to ruin my good time. I vowed then and there to make the most of the day. Take in the fresh mountain air. See new bits of sky. And when we got down I would march over to Drew and I would look him square in those stunning eyes and I would say, *Listen, I know that I'm not like a lot of other girls, but just give me some time. I have really kissable lips and a lot of other good qualities. Like I have a great sense of rhythm and I have 20/20 vision and I'm not bad at Ping-Pong and I can —*

Okay, maybe I'd come up with something shorter.

Ashley wanted to try the Basin Trail. She said it was supposed to be intermediate level, but there weren't too many turns and at the bottom there was a basin with a little pond and sometimes kids from the neighborhood went ice-skating there.

"We have to walk a little ways to get there, but I promise it's supposed to be tote delish." Sounded good to me.

We made our way to the head of the trail and pushed off. I leaned forward, bending my knees, nose pointed straight ahead.

"Woo-hoo!" I heard Ashley yell below me.

"Woo-hoo!" I yelled back, the wind whipping my face. It felt great. My legs felt solid and sturdy. I followed the trail carefully, taking in deep breaths, smelling the firs, the bark, the cold. And then we emptied out into a beautiful opening. There was a circular pond, slick and white, with a handful of kids slipping and tripping around in lopsided circles. There were two mothers standing by the side, watching.

"So cute," sighed Ashley.

"Mmm-hmmm," I agreed.

"They look so *free*," she said.

"Yeah. Yeah."

We stood there and just watched. It felt so good and therapeutic to see their little bodies flailing and flopping, weebling and wobbling. They were having so much fun. They didn't care what they looked like or if they were cool or if they were supposed to be something that they weren't. They were just *being*. I had a lot to learn from them. I needed to just be okay with me the way that I was.

Chapter 12

Okay. One thing I'm not good at is waiting.

I was sitting in the living room of the inn at 11:00 that night, staring at my cell phone, which was *still* not ringing. Hadn't Phoebe said that she would call me or I would call her, but that some way we would talk tonight? What was *with* her? I felt like I was going to go nuts just sitting in front of the fire all night. And I didn't want to go outside and go for a walk, because I was kind of expecting another call, too, on the land line. Only it was pretty obvious at this point that that wasn't going to happen. But I promised myself I wouldn't give up hope. Not yet, at least.

This is what happened. That afternoon, I had seen

Drew leaving the chalet just as I was returning my skis. I ran after him.

"Hey!" (Me: panting, smiling brightly, determined.)

"Hey." (Him: blank face, eyes shifty, but still frustratingly handsome.)

"Are you on your way somewhere?" (Me: still smiling, still determined.)

"Yup." (Him: uninterested, taking out a ChapStick.)

"Well, I'd love to talk, if you want." (Me: trying to remember global warming, nuclear proliferation, everything else more important and sadder than this moment.)

"Sure, yeah. Listen, I'm late." (Him: walking away.)

"Well, do you want my number maybe?" (Me: determined. Not to cry.)

"I'll just call the inn. I've got the number there . . ." (Him: disappearing into the dark, his voice trailing off, leaving me shivering and cold.)

So I came back to the inn, crushed and hollow. Ashley asked me if I wanted to go back to the hotel where she was staying and watch movies with her and Emily, but I told her I was pretty tired. Which was true. I was tired of wondering. And wishing. And *waiting*.

I tried Phoebe a bunch of times again before giving up and settling on the couch in the living room. It was pretty quiet there, actually. Jeremy and Aaron had gone out with some other guys to hear a local band, and Dad and Kathy had gone to bed early. There were a couple of other guests hanging around the fire and I briefly saw Eric and Phil cleaning up after supper, but besides that, I was mostly by myself, trying to figure out what I was going to say when (or if) either phone rang. So far, nothing. Except for one time I came back from the bathroom and there was a copy of *Franny and Zooey* on the couch where I had been sitting. I guess Eric had put it there. Which was bizarre, right? That guy was hard to figure out. I actually tried opening it and reading, but all the words kept swimming around in front of me.

11:28. The phone next to me started vibrating.

"Pheebs!"

"Hey, Sam."

"Okay, *what* is going on?"

"Sorry, it's been really busy here. You know, my cousin Amy is staying with us for a few days." I had forgotten about that. Phoebe's cousin Amy is really cool. She's two years older than us and lives in Seattle and loves to go to the movies and shopping and stuff. But still, it didn't seem like Amy would stop Phoebe from calling me.

"Well, so what have you been doing? Seen any movies or anything?" I tried to sound relaxed and chatty, but I felt like I was going to split in half, I was so uneasy.

"Not really," she said. "What's going on with you?"

"Nothing." Two could play at that game, right? Only it felt really stupid and mean. And I was dying to tell her about everything with Drew and Liz, and Ashley, but mostly Drew. It was so horrible just sitting here in this empty space.

Please, just say something. Anything.

I heard her take in a long breath.

"Actually, Sam, I guess there is something I want to say. I was gonna talk to you about it when you got home but . . ." She trailed off.

"Please, Pheebs. It's me, your best friend. What is it? Is everything okay?" Another thing I am not good at is surprises. And this one didn't sound like tickets to the circus or a new puppy.

"Yeah. No, everything's fine. I just wanted to say . . . Well, I'm really glad you said that thing the other night about being over Leo because, um . . ."

"Phoebe, you were so right. Even though things are

not so great with Drew right now, I know that Leo is *not* who I should be with. I mean, there is so much more out there. Like people who can talk and laugh and — no, wait, I interrupted. Sorry. What were you saying?"

"Well, it's just . . ." Another deep breath. "I've seen him a lot at Murphy's the past few nights and . . . I kinda know that he has feelings for another girl," she said.

"Wow!" Okay, not what I wanted to hear but I had other men to think about, right? Still, I felt my chest tighten. "How did you find that out?"

"Because he told me."

"Well, whatever. That's good, I guess. Do you know who it is? Is it that girl Dana? I think she got a nose job. Or is it Emma Parker, the girl from Central?"

Silence.

And it took me a few seconds, but then I knew exactly who that girl was. My words hung in the air. My mouth was still open, and my breath was really fast and loud.

"It's me," Phoebe mumbled. It was the softest voice, barely above a whisper. But it didn't matter. I didn't need her to be any louder.

"Sam?"

"Yeah?"

"I don't want to do anything about it unless you are

really over him. I mean, he told me the other night at Dave's, and I told him I had to think about it, because I wanted to talk to you first, but then it didn't feel right to tell you over the phone, you know? So I just tried to ignore it until you came home. But then tonight he was, like, 'Well, what do you think?' and I didn't know what to say because I like him, you know we both liked him, but I would never *ever* do anything to jeopardize our friendship, but then the other night you said you were completely over him and then you said it again tonight, but . . . okay, that's it."

It felt like all the air had been knocked out of me. "Did you . . . kiss?" I asked. I knew it was immature. But I didn't care.

"Well, no," she said. "I mean, sort of, but —"

That was more than I needed to know, actually.

"What do you mean, *sort of*?! You can't *sort of* kiss someone, Phoebe! Just like you can't *sort of* be someone's best friend! Which, I guess, is what you've been doing!"

"No, Sam! That's not true! You *are* my best friend! You always have been! That's why —"

I opened the sliding door and stepped outside so I could really scream now. It was freezing out here, but

I didn't care. I was sweating, and I could feel the blood pulsing behind my eyes.

"Yeah, well, you know what, Phoebe? Best friends don't do things like this! They don't go behind backs and start kissing people and lying to them over the phone —"

"I didn't lie, Sam!"

"No! You don't get to talk right now, Phoebe! This is my turn to talk and you'd better sit down because you know when I get going it's gonna be a long night! I can't believe this is happening! I can't believe you would think that was okay! I trusted you! I told you everything!"

The tears started leaking out. More like gushing, actually. And I didn't try to stop them. I was so mad and hurt and lost and alone. Everyone was abandoning me. First my dad, then stupid Drew, and now my best friend in the whole world. I think Phoebe was crying, too. I couldn't really tell. But when I finally caught my breath, I could hear her making those gulpy hiccuping sounds and sniffling a lot.

"I'm gonna go," I whimpered.

"No, wait! Sam, I'm gonna tell him I can't see him anymore. I swear. I didn't mean to —"

"You do whatever you want, Phoebe," I said and closed my phone.

I pulled my sweater in tighter around me. My fingers were numb from the cold and I looked up into the sky. That wide-open infinite sky. But now I didn't know what to ask for anymore.

Chapter 13

The next day, I knew I looked like a train wreck — my nose and eyes were red and swollen and I had those little splotches on my cheeks that I get after a long bawl. Ashley didn't say anything, though, she just grabbed my hand as I was picking up my skis and said, "Hey, friend. What should we do today?"

It was her last day in West Lake. Emily was still stuck in bed, and Ashley said she wanted to go on as many trails as she could before the day was through. I told her I could show her Pine Bluffs. She was game. The whole way up, she told me stories about these chickens on her farm called Lucy and Desi. They always fought with each other and pecked at each other's feathers until they had big bald spots. And she had a dog named Echo who was part German shepherd and blind in one eye and always tried to push all the furniture into one corner of the living room.

By the time we got to the top, I wasn't exactly laughing, but I was feeling a little lighter. And I was glad I hadn't stayed at the inn sulking.

We did Pine Bluffs.

"Woo-hoo!" Ashley yelled.

"Woo-hoo," I answered, even though it sounded pretty weak.

Then we tried Mountain Vista Trail, which had amazing mountain vistas (duh). And one called Western Ridge, which I guess was on the west side of the mountain range. To be honest, I wasn't looking that much at the views today. I was concentrating more on yelling and yodeling with Ashley the whole way down. And I was going pretty fast now. I leaned lower and really caught some speed.

"Tote fabu!" she drawled at the bottom of our fourth run of the morning. "Man, I could use some grub!"

"Me, too." I knew there was a good chance that I would see Drew at the chalet, but I had to face him sometime, right? I still wasn't sure what I was going to say, but I would cross that bridge when I came to it.

I picked out a slice of pizza and a cup of chicken noodle soup and put down my tray of food next to Ashley's. She had gotten a meatball sub and a side of mozzarella sticks. Yeah, I liked this girl. We got each other. Dad, Kathy, and Jeremy found us. Jeremy's face was bright red and his freckles looked like they were on fire. He had gone snowboarding in some canyon out past the Basin.

"Greatest morning ever!" he announced, his mouth full of chicken Parmesan. I rolled my eyes at Ashley and we both laughed. All during lunch we chatted about food, school, life in Texas. Ashley was charming the pants off Dad. I could tell he was glad to see I had made a good friend out here. She told us she was from a little town called Lubbock. Her dad was a farmer and she had four older brothers. Her mom was a secretary at their church.

"What church do y'all go to?" she asked.

I saw Jeremy laugh into his sandwich.

"Actually, we're Jewish," I said.

"That is awesome! We have a couple of Jewish kids in my school. Ari Nussbaum and Peter — something. They read a lot! Do y'all read a lot, too?"

Now I laughed. So did Dad and Kathy. To a total

stranger, I bet it looked like we were one big happy family. I wasn't about to explain.

After lunch, Ashley and I headed back out to the slopes.

"See you suckers later," said Jeremy. Aaron was waiting for him with some of their new buddies from snowboarding class.

"Usual time? At the chalet?" asked Dad.

"Sure," I said.

"Ashley, it was a pleasure. Hope to see you later."

"Thanks, Mr. and Mrs. Levy. You take care now," she said with her endearing smile.

Yeah. Keep the mouth shut, Levy. Not worth it.

I watched Dad and Kathy take hands and head off to the cross-country trails. Then Ashley and I got in line for the lift. Ashley was talking about how sweet my family was, and how it was so funny that the cheese here tasted different than the cheese in Texas, but that made sense, didn't it? Because it was different milk or at least different cows, right? And I think I said sure, but to be honest, I was having trouble concentrating now because a few feet behind us I could hear, "No, you're doing great, doll. You just have to remember —"

"Keep your behind *behind*. I know. I was trying, but I just couldn't get it. Oops!" *Giggle giggle.*

Well, I guess it was time to cross that bridge. I needed to get a good look, though, just to make sure. I tried to act really subtle, like I had gotten something on my shoulder, craning my neck around to wipe off an imaginary dust ball. Yup. Light blue hooded jacket with fuzzy white trim, and a matching fuzzy scarf that was sprouting out of her neck. She looked cute enough. Small. Upturned nose. And right next to her was that shock of blond hair.

"That's all right. We'll get some time up there just you and me this afternoon," Drew said.

I felt my jaw tighten. My hands were balled up into fists.

"Sammy, what do you think?" Ashley was saying.

I turned back around. "Um, I think . . ."

"Wow! The Olympics! Are you for real? That is so totally awesome and inspiring!" Fuzzy yammered behind me.

"Weeeellllll?" said Ashley.

"Yeah, well. It was only the trials. I'm hoping next time — you know, I'll actually get to compete," he said, and I could just imagine his lips stretching into that seductive grin.

"You okay, darlin'?" asked Ashley. Her voice was soft and concerned now. "You look a little pale."

"Yeah. Um, Ashley, I think there's something I have to do before I can go up again. Is that okay?"

"Sure! I thought you just went after lunch, though. Oh, well. Whatever. Sometimes I think that I've gone all the way and then as soon as I zip my pants up I have to go again. I think a lot of girls are like that. I try to drink a lot of cranberry juice. I heard that's good for your kidneys. I don't know. Have you ever tried it?"

"No, I just have to talk to someone. About . . . something." I really didn't want to go into it. I didn't want to be doing this at all. But I knew I had to do it now. Before I lost my nerve.

"Well sure, Sam," Ashley said. "You do what you need to do."

"Be right back." I dug my poles firmly into the ground and shook my hair out behind me. I marched over toward him. Or rather, I skidded. It's kind of hard to do anything else on skis.

"Um, Drew?"

His face turned around slowly. Like he was taking his time. Like he had been expecting me.

"Hey, what's up, Sam?"

"Well, I was just wondering if maybe we could talk or something?"

"Sure, what about?"

Fuzzy Wuzzy was playing with her zipper, but I could tell she was listening.

"Um, I mean, maybe we could talk somewhere else?"

"Well, I'm kinda busy right now," he said, shrugging his shoulders. There were just a few people left ahead of him now in line.

You can do this, Levy.

"No, I know. Not now. I meant, like after your . . ." I looked at Fuzzy. "Your *class*. Maybe we could grab some hot chocolate?"

He sighed.

"Hmm, I've got plans already."

"Really?" I sounded like someone had just punched me in the gut. Maybe because that's what it felt like, too.

"Yeah," he said.

"Are your plans . . . all night?" Ugh. This was not

how I had envisioned it at all. Fuzzy was practicing sticking her behind behind.

"Sam?! We're up!" It was Ashley. The chair was coming toward her. I looked at Drew. His eyes were clear and totally blank.

"Just go on up!" I called to her.

"You sure?" she hollered back.

"Yeah, I'll meet you up —"

"Whoa! Okeydoke! See ya up there, darlin'!" I heard, and then I saw her honey-colored braids swinging up in the air. Who was that next to her? It looked like an older man with gray hair. Why had I done that to Ashley? Especially after she'd been so good to me. I never wanted to be someone who chose a guy over a friend. That would be like — and now my chest tightened even more. That would be like Phoebe.

"Um, Sam?" said Drew. "We're gonna be up in a sec, too. So, was there something else you wanted to say or are we done here?"

Are we done here? I felt my nostrils flaring.

"No," I said. "Actually, there is something."

"Okay, well . . ."

I took a deep breath, puffed out my chest, and said,

"Drew, I know you're a busy man and you need to give a private lesson to Fuzzy here, but you should think about what you're doing, because I was totally into you and I thought you were into me but if this is just about me not wanting to have sex then that's really immature. There's a lot more to a relationship than just sex, you know? There's cuddling and conversation and just hanging out and being in the same moment together. And one day I'm gonna have sex, too, with someone I truly love. Yes, maybe it'll be when I'm forty-eight, but that's fine with me. Well, I hope it's before then, but whatever. The point is, you made a really stupid, shallow mistake and your Jetta smells like gym shoes."

No, I didn't say that.

I did take a deep breath. And then I did try to puff up my chest. And then I looked him in those icy eyes, and I said, "You should try reading more than just *Sports Illustrated*."

Then I dug my poles into the ground, summoned up all my strength, and pushed off as hard as I could.

Chapter 14

The only thing about trying to make a dramatic exit on skis is that there is no graceful way to do it. At least not the way I ski. I lifted my feet up, turned my body, and then thrust myself right into —

"Hey!"

"Hey." It was Eric. Awesome. Just who I wanted to see. I had managed to avoid him at the slopes the whole week until now, but of course it was the perfect time to run into him.

"Where are you off to in such a hurry?" he asked.

"Nowhere. Nothing. Sorry I knocked into you." I tried to move past him, but he stopped me with his hand.

"Hey, no worries. You heading up?" He pointed to the ski lift. I could've lied, I guess. I looked behind him.

The line of people waiting wound all the way to the chalet now. I could just imagine standing there, watching Drew and Fuzzy climb up into the sky, while I waited all alone. I looked back at Eric. The choices were dismal and dismaller.

"Yeah, I guess so," I said glumly.

"Mind if I join you?" He just didn't get it, did he? I was seriously regretting telling Ashley to head off. Along with a lot of other things I'd done in the past half hour.

"Whatever," I mumbled, pushing forward in the line.

"Yow! No fair! You're making it rock!" squealed Fuzzy as she and Drew started sailing up, her scraggly scarf trailing behind them. Wasn't there a way that thing could get caught in the chair and choke her? Just a little bit?

Eric and I moved forward silently. At least he wasn't trying to strike up a conversation. I didn't know who I hated more right now, Eric for warning me about Drew being a player, or Drew for proving him right. How could he have looked at me so coolly, like I was a complete stranger? Like he hadn't been trying to undo my jeans just the other night? I watched his blond head get smaller in the sky. I bet his hair was dyed. And

P.S. — cherry ChapStick was definitely for girls. I sighed. Most of all I hated myself right now, for falling for him.

The lift came toward us, and Eric and I got on. I felt my teeth grind together as we slowly inched up the side of the mountain.

And then, just as we were getting close to the top, Eric said, "Listen, Sam, I feel like I was kinda out of line when I said that stuff about Drew the other night . . ."

"Yeah, I don't really want to talk about this right now."

"No, we don't have to talk about it. I just wanted to say it was none of my business. I'm sorry. I really am. But I wouldn't have said it if —"

"If it wasn't true?" I finished.

"No, if —"

"Listen, Eric. You were right. Is that what you want to hear? Because you were. He's up there right now about to give some other girl a private tutorial and I'm pretty sure that involves getting in his Jetta tonight or finding some hot tub, and I'm the fool, once again. So there! You were right. I was wrong. Are you happy now?"

His mouth was hanging open a little. "No. No, I'm not happy," he said. "I didn't mean to make you feel —"

But there was no time for him to finish. We were

already at the top of the slope. We both lifted our skis and let go, coasting forward and then plowing to a stop, right next to the signs for the different trails.

I turned toward Devil's Canyon. I knew it was supposed to be one of the hardest trails, but I didn't care. I needed some speed. Some wind in my face. I needed to get away. Eric grabbed my arm.

"Wait, Sam. Hey, I'm really sorry that happened to you. I didn't tell you about Drew because I wanted you to — just, I'm sorry he did that to you."

"Well, don't worry about it. It's over now," I said, and without waiting a breath, I shoved off as hard as I could. I was flying, pulling through turns, hopping over dips, careening down the mountainside, bending my knees low and pushing into the wind.

I screamed. I bellowed. I didn't care who heard me. I didn't care what anybody thought of me. I was free! I was going to forget the whole world and I was going to conquer this slope. I tore through the snow, slipping and dipping and sliding and racing. Snaking through a patch of trees, swerving around a small hill, and then a mound of powdery-looking snow.

"Saaaam! Hold on!" I heard Eric calling behind me, but I ignored him. I didn't need him. I didn't need him or Drew or anyone. All I needed was me and the sky. I lifted both poles high in the air and stood up tall. I wanted to feel every inch of my body touch the air.

"Yoweeeeeeee!" I yelled.

And then something shifted. The ground was coming toward me. The trees were leaning sideways and my skis were going forward but the rest of my body wasn't catching up to them. I tried to plow to a stop but my left leg was sliding out and my right one was going in the opposite direction, and then the next thing I knew I was slipping backward. The trees came toward me, the sky came toward me, the yellow yolk of sun was falling on me, and then I hit earth. Hard. I felt my teeth knock together and all the air escape from my chest and then everything went dark.

Chapter 15

"Sam! Sam! Can you hear me?"

I opened my eyes, and the sky was green. A deep jade with little flecks of yellow. No, wait. A thin nose poked out in between. It was . . . ?

"Hey," Eric said softly. His ears were bright red from the cold.

"Your ears are cold," I heard myself saying, and he started to laugh. His eyes were still wide and worried, though.

"You okay?" he asked.

"Yeah, I think so."

"I'm gonna call ski patrol," he said.

"No, no! Please don't." I didn't feel like getting poked and prodded by those guys in bright orange snowsuits I had seen flying by. I could wiggle all my fingers and toes. Nothing felt broken. I just needed time to lie there for a minute or two.

"Does anything hurt?"

"I don't think so. Just my head." My tongue was thick and fuzzy. It felt like someone was squeezing my brain.

"What about if I just —"

"Whoa!" said Drew, flying in next to me, his skis shaving off snow right into my face. "That was a doozy, huh?"

"I'm okay." I wasn't quite sure of that, but I really wanted him to go away.

Drew looked me up and down. "Well, let me see," he said.

"I was gonna call the ski patrol . . ." Eric started.

Drew ignored him. "Does this hurt?" he said, taking one of my legs and giving it a little shake. I couldn't look at him. It was too weird having him touch me like this. I remembered how gentle his hands were before. Now I felt like a head of iceberg lettuce in the produce aisle.

"Sam?" Drew said.

"No, it's fine," I said.

"This?" He shook the other.

"Nope."

"Uh, okay, how many fingers am I holding up?" He put up three. This was ridiculous.

"You don't have to do this," I said, rolling my eyes. Ow, that hurt.

"Okay, well then, can you get up? Because we really should get out of the middle of the trail."

"Yeah, okay. Fine." Anything to get him out of here.

He started pulling me up by the arm. I tried to follow, but it felt like my legs were made of lead. I couldn't get my feet to plant themselves. The ground started tilting back and forth, and everything turned bright pink. My stomach lurched forward and my head felt like it was on backward, and before I knew it, I was crumpling down to my knees, and my lunch was coming out all over the snow.

"Ew! Nasty!" said Drew, backing away.

"All right, just give her a sec," came another voice. The pink slowly started separating, the trees were turning green again, the snow, white. And now I felt someone gently easing me back down to the ground.

"Thanks," I whispered.

"Sure," said Eric. "You want to just sit here for a bit?"

It was too late. The orange men were here.

"Hey, how's it going? You take a spill?"

"What hurts?"

"Anything hurt?"

"You know what year it is?"

"Who's the president?"

"How many fingers am I holding up?"

The two of them talked so fast over each other that I felt dizzier than before.

"That's okay, really, I'm fine," I said, when they both paused for a breath.

"Okay."

"All right."

"You sure?"

"She said she was fine."

"All right. But if you need anything, just give a holler." And they sped off.

Whew. Now all I needed was for Drew and Eric to follow them.

"Hey, guys? Thanks for stopping by, but really, I think I'm okay," I said.

"You sure?" said Drew, still staring at the spot where I had thrown up in the snow.

"Yeah."

"Okay. Feel better!" I heard him call before he took off. Jerk.

Eric squatted back down next to me.

"Sorry, I know I'm not your favorite person, but I'm not leaving so fast," he said.

"Really, I'm fine."

"I promise I'll leave you alone once we get down the mountain, but first let's just stay here for a little bit, okay?"

I didn't really have the energy to argue. Plus I wasn't quite sure what would come out of my mouth if I opened it again.

So we sat. The cool air felt good now. I was mostly just spacing out, trying to make the trees calm down and stand straight. A couple of times I heard the whoosh and whir of skis coming down the slope behind us, but Eric always stood up and waved his hands, directing people out of the way before they got near us. I guess most of the people who tried Devil's Canyon were more experienced skiers.

I don't know how long we were there, but at some point I realized that my butt was getting really soggy and cold.

"Hey, I think I'm ready to get going," I said.

"You sure?" asked Eric.

"Yup. Yeah."

"Okay, well, we could either call to get you a stretcher, or we can walk down the rest of the way," he said.

I shuddered. Stretchers terrify me.

"It's not that far from here, but I don't know how steady you feel."

"I'll walk," I said.

"Okay, let's just take it slow." He wrapped one arm around my shoulders and rested the other on my waist, pulling me up slowly, carefully.

"Is that okay?" he said quietly.

"Yeah." I really meant to say, "No, thanks," but at that moment I was so grateful to have him there. He was strong, too.

"Anytime you need to stop and take a break, just let me know, okay? Easy does it. And here we go."

His hands stayed securely attached to my shoulder and waist as we shuffled forward. It took us a year to get down the rest of the way, I swear. Eric was doing most of the work, steering me cautiously, thoughtfully. He told me stories about all of his injuries on the slopes. He had broken his nose three times. Two times on trees.

Once on his own knee. I started to laugh, but it hurt my head too much when I did.

Just past the chalet where we got our lunch and rented skis, there was another wooden hut with a red cross on it and a shuttered window. I had never noticed it before. There was just one room inside with a cot, a chair, a desk, and a counter full of bottles of antiseptics and cotton balls. A sweet-looking older man sat at the desk in a white lab coat over a thick green sweater. He had a gray beard and reading glasses perched on the end of his nose, and he was very intently filling out a crossword puzzle when we came in.

"Took a spill, huh?" he asked with a warm smile. His voice sounded like static on the radio, deep and crackly.

"Yup," I said.

"Hi, I'm Dr. Wasserman."

"Sam Levy."

"You mind if I step out for a second and get someone to help me find your dad?" asked Eric.

"That's okay, you don't have to."

"Good idea," said Dr. Wasserman at the same time. Eric left before I could protest.

I explained what happened as Dr. Wasserman sat me down on the little cot and checked the back of my head for any lumps or bumps. Then he pulled gingerly on all of my limbs.

"You stop me if anything hurts," he said. He touched my glands, massaged my stomach, listened to my chest and took all my vitals. He shined a little penlight in my ears, my throat, my eyes.

"Anybody home?" he said with a gruff laugh. He smelled like cough drops.

Just then, Dad burst through the door. "Oh! Sammy! You okay, sweetie?"

"I'm fine, Dad. I'm fine."

He rushed in and kissed me on the forehead. I could see Kathy behind him, nervously craning her neck.

"Are you sure? Are you sure?" Dad was asking, frantically running his hands over my face, my neck, my arms.

"She's gonna be fine," said Dr. Wasserman.

"Oh, sorry," said Dad. "I'm Judd Levy, Sam's dad."

"Eugene Wasserman."

"And I'm Kathy," I heard. Good job. No further explanation needed.

Dr. Wasserman turned back to me. "Well, the bad news is, you took quite a spill. The good news is, I think you're gonna live. You probably have a mild concussion.

I could send you over to Burlington General to get a checkup, but there isn't really much they can do for you except tell you to rest. Or you could just go back to wherever you're staying and put your feet up by the fire for a day or two. What do you think?"

"I can take you to the hospital if you want. I've got the truck," said Eric. I had forgotten that he was still there.

"Oh, you're staying at Phil's place?" asked Dr. Wasserman.

"Yeah," said Dad. "Listen, Sam, we can go to the hospital if you want, sweetie."

"Whatever will make you feel better," Kathy chimed in.

"Well, you've got a big fan club here, huh?" said Dr. Wasserman. "What do you think, young lady?"

"I think sitting in front of the fire sounds good," I replied.

"You sure?" Dad asked.

"Yeah."

Dr. Wasserman told me to get in a lot of clear fluids like broth, and if I threw up again or felt really dizzy to give him a call. He helped me off the table and gave me his card.

"Seriously, anytime. My usual activity for a Wednesday night is to watch water come to a boil or time the traffic lights, so don't hesitate to get in touch with me." Then he turned to the three faces in the doorway.

"Now, who is going to take this lovely lady home?" he asked.

"I will," said Dad and Eric at the same time.

"It's okay, I've got her," said Dad.

"Really, I can take her, Mr. Levy," said Eric. "You guys only have a few days left on the slopes. Why don't you finish your afternoon?"

"No, no, no, no, no, I'll take her."

"It's no trouble. My truck's parked right over there."

While they were talking, I took the opportunity to lie back down on the cot. My limbs were so achy and tired. So were my eyes.

The next thing I knew, Eric was easing me off of the cot, and we were saying good-bye to Dr. Wasserman. Dad and Kathy were going to find Jeremy and return all of our equipment.

"So, I guess I don't qualify for the Super G, huh?" I said as we walked slowly to the parking lot.

"The Super G?" asked Eric.

"Never mind." I was glad he didn't get it. "Sorry I was such an ass. I was just trying to . . . I don't know. I was being stupid, I guess."

"Hey, these things happen, you know?" said Eric.

"Sam!" I heard behind me. Eric helped me turn around. It was Ashley, running toward us with her hands in the air.

"I'm so sorry. I tried waiting for you up there, but then I thought I missed you. And then when I got to the bottom I looked for you again. And then Drew came by and told me what happened. Oh sweetie, are you okay?"

"Yeah, Ashley. I'm all good."

"We were having such a fun time, too. Tote bum." Which I guessed meant "total bummer." I tried to give her a smile. She smiled back.

"Oh, darlin', can I do anything for you? Do you need anything?"

Her face looked so long with concern.

"That's okay, Ashley. Really, I just need to go back to the inn and lie down."

"Okay. Well, how about I try to catch up with

you later today on the phone, okay? We still have to exchange e-mail addresses or something so we can stay buds."

"That sounds good," I said.

"Ooooh, I'm gonna miss you. Can I . . . ?" She reached in to give me a hug. "You take care now, you hear?" She looked like she might cry.

"Promise. You, too." I wanted to tell her how much fun she was, but I didn't feel too steady standing up.

Eric and I walked the rest of the way in silence. His truck was a big navy pickup.

"This is Snoop," he said.

I looked around, but there was nobody there. "Who?"

"The truck. His name is Snoop."

"Oh hi, Snoop."

"Just to warn you? It's pretty hairy inside. Usually I'm traveling with someone much smaller and furrier." He smiled.

"No problem," I said.

He helped me up into the cab and made sure I was all settled in before he shut the door. There were a lot of dog hairs in here. And pine needles on the floor. And on the console I saw there was a small pad of paper with what looked like a sketch of a mountain pass, the rocks drawn in shades of gray. I didn't have time to get a good look, though. Eric was already opening his door.

"I swear it'll warm up in just a few. You freezing?" he asked.

"Nah, I'm fine."

He turned the key in the ignition, and Steely Dan was playing really loud.

"Oops, sorry about that," he said sheepishly, ejecting the CD. The local news came on.

"Looks like it's gonna be a big one, too. Starting off in the morning and not tapering off until late in the evening. We may get as much as one and a half to two feet, so get out those shovels," said the announcer.

Eric turned the radio down.

"Sounds like it might be the perfect day to stay in tomorrow," he said.

I didn't even answer. I just leaned back into the headrest and closed my eyes.

By the time Dad and Kathy and Jeremy came back, Eric had already set me up in front of the fire in the living room with a fleece blanket that felt like butter and a steaming cup of hot chocolate. I wasn't sure I could get it down, but it smelled great.

"How's the patient?" asked Dad, kissing me on the forehead.

"Better," I murmured.

"We found someone who wanted to see you," said Kathy.

"Nice job, nerd," said Jeremy, leaning in and rubbing my head delicately.

"Sorry they brought you back, Jer." My words kind of mushed all together, I was so relaxed and sleepy now.

"Whatever. I was done. Just get some rest," he said.

The rest of the afternoon I spent in and out of sleep. I think I started to drink my hot chocolate about four different times, but I never made it very far. Each time I woke up, there was a fresh cup there. Dad and Kathy camped out on one of the other couches reading, and every once in a while when I woke up, one of them was hovering over me, just watching. At some point, Dad came into view with his cell phone in his hand.

"Hey, chicken, can you talk?" he asked, handing me the phone.

"Hello?"

"Mom!" It was so good to hear her voice.

"Oh honey, are you okay?"

"Mom, don't worry, I'm fine."

"That's what your father said, but I just wanted to hear it from you."

"I am, Mom. I am."

"You know he called me first thing. It was so nice of him. And I was thinking I hadn't talked to you in a while but I didn't want to bug you on your honeymoon — I mean, their honeymoon, but . . . ah, I miss you, Sam," she said quietly now.

"Yeah, Mom. I miss you, too." She sounded so lonely.

"Okay," said Mom, back to her cheerful patter. "It's just a few days. I'll see you soon. You get some rest now, you hear?"

"Yes, Mom."

"I'm serious. Do not pass Go. Do not collect two hundred dollars." That's what Mom always says when she wants you to do something right away, like wash the dishes or take out the garbage. It's from the game Monopoly.

"Got it," I said, smiling.

"I love you, chicken."

"Love you, too, Mom."

I handed the phone back to Dad.

"I guess I should've asked you before I called her, but I knew she would want to know. Sorry, kiddo," he said.

"No, I'm glad you did. It was good to hear her voice."

"Yeah, yeah, it was," said Dad. And I realized how lucky I was that they were still friends. That they really did try to keep us a family somehow.

Just then, Eric came in with another cup of cocoa.

"Hey!" he said. "I didn't know you were up. You look a lot better."

"Doesn't she?" said Dad.

Then they both just stood there, looking at me. So I said, "What did I miss?"

"Nothin'," said Eric. "Oh, actually, you got a phone message."

"Huh?"

"Let me see if I got this right." He cleared his throat, then started again in a sugary singsong: "Please tell Sam that it was *tote* hilare hangin' out with her and I hope she gets better soon. And we *have* to stay in touch. I think it'd be super-fun to be PPs because nobody does that anymore. Okay, toodles!"

Dad gave him a small round of applause.

"Wait — PPs?" I asked.

"Pen pals?" Eric shrugged. "She gave me her address, too."

"Right."

And now I saw that the lamp next to me was on, and the room had softened into a bluish gray. There were a bunch of guests from the inn crowded into the lobby, and some heading into the dining room, too.

"Hey, is it happy hour already?" I asked, sitting up.

"Yeah, but I don't suggest that you drink right now," Dad said, smiling.

"Thanks, Dad. No, I meant, sorry I'm still in the middle of everything."

"No worries," said Eric.

"Oh, yay! You're up!" Kathy came in then, with two cocktails in her hands. She handed one to Dad. Her cheeks were really flushed, and she looked like she was swaying a little.

"To Sam!" she said, raising her glass. And then her

eyes got big and watery. “We’re really, really grateful that you’re okay,” she said. Her voice was trembling. She looked down quickly.

“Hey, thanks,” I said. I looked down, too.

But out of the corner of my eye, I saw Eric slip out of the room.

Chapter 16

My favorite moment of any movie is when everything goes dark, just before the first image, and the music begins. It's only a breath — less than a second, but it always sends shivers up my spine.

After dinner, Phil and Eric had rearranged the living room for Classic Movie Night. They put the couches in a semicircle and pulled out a big screen. The first one was going to be Hitchcock's *North by Northwest*. The second one was going to be something about snow. I was planning on being asleep by then, anyway. Everyone settled into their spots. It seemed like it was mostly couples except for me — Dad and Kathy, Dara and Stevie D., a couple of other twosomes I'd seen at breakfast. Jeremy was upstairs watching some heavyweight fight. And then there was me, tucked into a corner of one of the armchairs. That was okay. I wasn't in the mood for cuddling, except for maybe a couch pillow. But just as I was sinking back, letting my eyes grow heavy again, I felt a vibrating in my sweatshirt pocket. My cell phone. I must've looked like a frog, jumping in my seat. The couple next to me jumped, too.

The caller ID said PHEEBS. Should I take it? I didn't know what I had to say to her. I didn't really want to tell her about my concussion or the Drew saga and I certainly didn't want to hear about how important our friendship was.

The call went to voice mail, and I saw that I had eight missed calls. All from her. The phone started vibrating again. I could just see her waiting on the other end, twisting a red curl around her finger. Ugh. What was there to talk about?

C'mon, Levy. She was *your best friend just a few days ago.*

Weren't near-death experiences supposed to make you more humble and forgiving? What about clunks on the head? Before I could think about it too much, I wrapped a blanket around myself, put on my slippers, and crept toward the back of the room.

"You okay?" whispered Dad. Kathy was asleep on his shoulder.

"Yeah, yeah. Just getting some air," I whispered back.

I made it outside just as she was calling a third time.

"Hey, Phoebe."

"Sam! Wow! I didn't think that I would get you! I just — I just was trying in case — wow. I didn't know if you would pick up. Or if you wanted to talk or — am I interrupting you?" She was breathing so loud it felt like a tornado in my ear.

"No."

"It's really good to hear your voice! How are you? How's everything?"

"Good." Maybe I wasn't ready to have this conversation after all. I still felt so angry.

"What's going on?"

"Nothin'."

"You go skiing?"

"Yup."

"Was it cold?"

"Yup."

"How cold?"

This was stupid.

"Listen, Phoebe. I really don't feel like talking to

you but I picked up because I thought I should, but unless you have anything to say — no, actually I don't want to hear anything you have to say right now, so why are you calling?" My head was throbbing now and my jaw felt stiff and sore.

"I just wanted to know how *you* were, Sam. I mean, I don't want to talk about this stuff until you get home. I mean, it's over. But the point is, how are *you*?"

"Fine," I said blandly.

"But, really, I know things were hard with Kathy and then you said things were weird with Drew last time, and I just wanted to know what was up." She really was trying. I had to give her credit for that.

"Well, Kathy is still Kathy, and Drew and I broke up."

"You did? Why? What happened?!"

"Listen, Phoebe, I don't know if I feel comfortable talking to you about this right now. I mean, we wanted different things. He only reads magazines. He said I talked too much. He really just wanted to get down my pants."

Then there was a few minutes of us just listening to each other breathe.

Until Phoebe said, "I'm sorry, Sam. I really am."

"Yeah, thanks," I said. I wanted to believe her. But I

was also done. "Hey, Phoebe, I'm gonna go back inside now. It's cold."

"Are you sure? I mean, I don't want you to get cold. But it's good to talk to you."

"Yeah, but I need to go. I'll be home on Sunday."

"Oh, no! We have to talk before then. I mean, if you want to."

"We'll see."

"Okay. Sam?"

"Yeah?"

"I love you." She sounded a little teary now. But I couldn't say it back. Not right now at least.

"Sorry, Pheebs. You're cutting out," I said. And then I hung up.

I drew my blanket in tighter around my shoulders and tucked my hands inside. It was cold out here, but I wasn't ready to leave this night quite yet. The moon peeking through the clouds, its beams flooding the snow with shafts of shimmering light. It was the first time my head had felt completely calm in a while.

And then, just ahead, out beyond the first small hill, I saw something dark zip across the white expanse. I pulled myself up on my toes to get a better look. It flickered across the snow again. It looked like maybe it was an animal of some kind. Were there wolves out here? Mountain lions? I should've read one of those magazines they had lying around more carefully. What kind of animals roamed the hills of Vermont? Maybe I needed to go back in after all. It would be just like me to get mauled by a mountain lion. And everybody would be too busy watching the movie to hear my screams. But I stood on my tiptoes again. I was fascinated. Yes, it was definitely an animal and it was racing back and forth across the lawn now, coming toward the inn. And then behind it, coming out of the darkness, I saw a human figure jogging through the snow.

"Hey!" said Eric, coming up to the porch, panting.

"Hey."

There was a stick in his hand and his dog was jumping up and down, trying to grab it from him.

"How you doing?"

"Good. Better. Thanks — for everything," I said.

"Ah, please. No worries. Whatcha doing out here?"

"I don't know. Just enjoying this night, I guess."

"Yeah, it is great, isn't it?" he said. "You can feel the storm coming. Can smell it in the trees." He gestured above his head.

The dog jumped up even higher.

"Hey, I don't think you two have formally met, have you?" asked Eric.

I shook my head no.

"Samantha, Fozzie. Fozzie, Samantha."

It was funny hearing him say my full name.

"Pleased to meet you, Fozzie," I said. Fozzie was still concentrating on the stick, leaping and standing on his hind legs.

"He says the pleasure is all his," said Eric. "Here, come here, boy!" He led Fozzie up onto the porch next to where I was standing. "Now, be a gentleman," Eric said, and he bent down to tap the wooden boards twice with the stick. Fozzie sat down and raised his right paw.

"He wants to shake your hand," Eric said. I bent down and took Fozzie's paw. He looked up at me with big, black, shiny eyes. His whiskers were drizzled with snow. I petted him behind the ears a little bit, and he licked my arm. Then Eric sent the stick sailing through the air.

"Go get it, boy!" he said, and Fozzie raced back into the snow, grabbed the stick, and galloped back toward us, his tail wagging furiously. He circled us up on the porch and then dropped the stick at my feet.

"I think he likes you," said Eric.

"He's not gonna like me once he sees how I throw," I said, picking up the stick. My head felt wonky when I bent down, and it took me a moment to readjust my balance once I stood up. But then I pulled my arm back and hurled the stick as far as I could. Which was only about twelve feet out in front of the porch. Fozzie looked at the stick lying in the snow, then looked back up at me.

"Sorry to disappoint you, Fozzie," I said.

"Nonsense. Go get it, Fozzie!" said Eric, and Fozzie ran out into the snow, grabbed the stick, and ran back, laying it at Eric's feet this time.

"Oooh, harsh," I said.

"Don't listen to him," said Eric. "He's just a dog." Then he picked up the stick and threw it out so far I couldn't see where it landed. Fozzie bounded out again.

"Hey, really. Thank you for taking care of me today," I said.

"Sure thing. How's the head?"

"Okay, a little wackadoo. But okay."

"Good, good."

"Listen, I feel like —"

"I just wanted to say —"

We were both talking at the same time.

"You go," he said.

"No, you go," I said.

"Really, you —"

"I just wanted to say sorry for yelling at you when we first met!" I burst out, and we both laughed. The corners of his eyes curled up when he laughed and now I saw he had really long eyelashes, too.

"Sam, you had every right to yell at me. I was butting my nose in where it wasn't needed," he said. "I just can't help it sometimes, you know? I mean, this thing is so huge." He tugged on his nose and laughed sheepishly.

"Well, you were right. Not just about Drew, but also, that first time you saw me, I was being pretty rough on Kathy — and she didn't deserve it."

"Right, Kathy," he said.

"She's my . . ." *Say it, Levy.* "Yeah, she's sorta my new stepmom."

Eric nodded. "They just got married, huh?"

"Yeah, last Saturday. This is like their honeymoon, only my brother Jeremy and I are here with them, which I think is kinda strange, but whatever. I think I was just giving her crap because she's not my mom and I'm kinda comparing her, or not really *comparing*, but I don't really — ugh, there I go again. See? Sometimes, if you haven't noticed, I don't know what to do, so I start talking and I just get carried away. You can tell me to shut up, you know that, don't you?"

Eric threw the stick back out for Fozzie.

"What if I don't want to?" he said.

"Well, I'll probably keep yapping away like I always do and sooner or later you're gonna wish you had," I said.

"Thanks, I'll keep that in mind." Eric smiled.

Huh. That was the first time anyone had said that to me.

"And just for the record," he continued, "I have mom issues, too. That's probably why I reacted so strongly. But it still wasn't cool of me." His voice got very quiet now, and even though I really wanted to ask him what he meant, I knew I shouldn't.

"Hey, um, so do you think you're going to go back to the slopes tomorrow?" he said eventually.

"I don't know, why?"

"Well, I'm no doctor, and again, I'm kinda butting my nose in your business, but I thought maybe you should take it easy."

"Yeah, I probably will." My head still felt pretty

heavy. I hadn't noticed it while I was talking to him, but now that he mentioned it . . .

"Fozzie and I will be around if you need anything. Although I promised him a good hike through the field."

"Sounds nice."

"Hey — you're welcome to join us, if you feel up for it," he said.

"Sure!" I volunteered before he was even done talking. And then I felt a little embarrassed. "I mean, sure," I said, a little softer.

"Great!" Eric said.

"Wait, do you need to ask Fozzie if that's okay? I don't want to intrude, you know."

"No, it was actually his idea to ask you," Eric replied.

"Well thanks, Fozzie," I said, looking up at the sky.

Chapter 17

"Now, are you sure you're going to be okay back here by yourself?" Dad was saying. He had both hands on my shoulders and he was studying my face carefully.

"Yes, Dad. I'll be fine." It was the third time that we were having this conversation this morning. Besides a slight headache and feeling super-thirsty, I really did feel a lot better. I even ate a huge breakfast of whole-wheat pancakes and fresh strawberries. Dad had watched me the whole time, probably waiting for me to explode or something.

"But I don't mind staying back here with you," he said now. "Jeremy and Kathy can go on, and you and I could veg out together in front of the fire. What do you say?" He tucked my hair behind my ear. Agh! I untucked it quickly, then took his hand.

"Dad, I'd feel bad if you stayed in. Really, I've got books to read and a stack of magazines."

"She's a big girl, Dad. Leave her alone," said Jeremy, heading toward the door.

"Okay, well, I'm bringing my cell phone with me and I'm keeping it on, so if you need anything at all, just give us a holler, okay?" Dad kissed me lightly on the forehead. Then Kathy stepped in.

"Seriously, Sam. Anything," she said. I saw Dad watching us apprehensively as she stood in front of me. She looked like she wanted to kiss me, too, but she wasn't sure if that was okay. I wasn't sure, either. So instead we just looked at each other, both kind of shifting our weight awkwardly.

Once they had left, I settled back in front of the fire. I had already showered and put on my clean jeans and my black turtleneck with my purple scarf. Yeah, it was kind of silly, but I was strangely looking forward to this walk with Eric and Fozzie. Of course, I hadn't seen either of them all morning, but I tried not to think about it too much. We hadn't set a time or anything. Or maybe they already took off before I got up.

Whatever, Levy — let it go.

"Man, everybody was doing their grocery shopping today. Must be the storm!" Eric came through the front door. He was carrying at least three paper bags full of groceries in each arm.

"Here, let me help!" I jumped up, but I guess I did it a little too quickly, and I got all of those little swimmy monsters in the sides of my vision. "Whoa," I heard myself say, as I reached out to balance myself with the back of my chair.

"No way, sickie." He smiled. "You okay?"

"Yeah, yeah."

"Here, let me just put this stuff away and then I thought we could head out past the Gallaghers' farm. There's a great trail over there that Fozzie loves. That is, if you're still up for it."

"Definitely." I followed him as he carried the packages through the dining room and into the kitchen.

"Great. Give me just ten minutes. It's already starting to come down out there. They originally said twelve to fourteen inches but now they're talking two feet or more. My dad went into Burlington today to take care of some business. I just hope he doesn't get stuck there."

As Eric talked, he pulled out bags of oats, bunches of fresh carrots, eggs, milk, sweet potatoes, and cheese. I looked around. The kitchen was huge, with a big industrial-sized cooking range and two deep metal sinks. There were pots and pans of every shape and size hanging from a rack over a big wooden block table in the middle, and there was the tallest spice rack that I had ever seen. I had never even heard of a lot of the spices in there.

An elderly couple came in carrying more groceries. The woman was wearing a blue-and-white-striped apron and had tight curls that were dyed somewhere between red and purple, and crinkly skin around small, deep-set eyes. The man was at least a foot shorter than her, and had olive skin, a head of full, dark hair, and a thick mustache to match.

"Oh, thanks guys," said Eric. "Martha, Luis. This is Sam. Sam, these are the two greatest cooks I know. They're the real reason why this place is still here."

The couple put down their packages, and Martha took one of my hands in hers. Her hands were amazing. They had big bulbous knuckles and a thousand wrinkles in them, roped with thick, green veins. She kneaded my palm like dough.

"What a pretty girl. Look at those eyes." Then she squeezed my fingers until I thought I might whimper a little. She turned to Luis.

"Luis, say hello."

He took my other hand. "Hello," he said with a shy smile. His accent was Italian? Spanish?

I learned that Martha and Luis had been the cooks for the Bishop Inn since it opened ten years ago. They lived one town over in Scudderville, and they had been married for forty-four years. I loved the way they finished each other's sentences and bickered over the tiniest things as they put the groceries away.

"What are you doing with that butter?"

"Putting it in the freezer like I always do."

"But don't put it in like that. Take it out of the box first."

"What does it matter?"

"Because when I go to get it I want to be able to grab one stick at a time, that's why."

"Why can't you separate it then?"

"Because I'm a busy lady, that's why. Just do what I say."

Luis swatted Martha on the butt. Eric crossed his eyes at me and smiled. I smiled back.

"Are you sure I can't help?" I asked.

"No, no, this is Luis's favorite thing to do. Right, Luis?" said Martha.

"Sure," he said and then when she turned around, he pretended to choke himself. I giggled. When they were done putting everything away, Eric filled a small bag with almonds and raisins for us. Then he took out some scraps of bacon from the top of the garbage and put them in a bag, too.

"You like bacon, right?" he said to me.

"Ummm . . ."

"Just kidding. It's for Fozzie, in case he gets too hungry," he explained.

"Now, be careful out there. It's coming down pretty thick," warned Martha as we put on our coats and boots.

"Thanks, Martha. We won't melt," Eric said, giving her a kiss on the cheek. "C'mon, boy!" he called, and then the three of us headed out the back door, with Fozzie leading the way.

The air felt crisp and alive with thick, fluffy flakes. We walked down the sloping backyard and then up over a slight hill. Fozzie was definitely in charge, racing around us, stopping to sniff through the snow and then doubling back, panting with excitement. Just over the hill we came to a small creek.

"Are you okay with this?" asked Eric, looking back at me as he stepped onto a smooth, flat rock.

"Sure," I said, following him carefully.

On the other side of the creek, we went up a small bank that led into a big field. Eric explained that this was part of the Gallaghers' farm. They grew corn and wheat in the summer and pumpkins in the fall. They also kept two horses, three pigs, a cow, and a family of chickens. The animals were all in the barn now, but when it was warmer out, Eric liked to come over and feed them leftover bread and carrots at night. The Gallaghers knew he came by. They always left the outside light on for him. We walked through the field and past the farmhouse, which looked like a small saltbox with wooden shingles and a bright red front door. Then Eric showed me how to squirm under a couple of loose boards in the fence. Fozzie knew the drill already, of course. Then up around another small hill.

The whole time, the snow was coming down in fat, downy flakes. But I barely noticed. I was too busy taking in the amazing views, the cold air. And of course, I was talking. It was really easy to talk to Eric about anything and everything. It felt effortless. He asked me about where I grew up in New York. I told him about life in the suburbs. How I went to public school, but still felt pretty sheltered, like everybody was kind of from the same social stratum. We all wound up wearing the same clothes, listening to the same music. Eric said he knew what that was like, living in West Lake for most of his life. He couldn't imagine living anywhere else, but he was going to be a senior next year and he was looking to go away for art school after that. We talked about our favorite musicians, our favorite authors. He was a big fan of Thoreau. I admitted I'd never read him before. Sometimes we walked for a really long time not saying anything at all, and that was easy, too.

And then, I don't know what made me do it, but at one point I just came out and said, "So what are these mom issues you have? I mean, is that okay if I ask?"

"Um . . ." his voice faded.

"No, never mind. That was nosy of me," I said.

"No. Hey, I've done my share of nosing around your life."

And then I heard him give a small sigh.

"Actually, well . . . my mom died two years ago. In a drunk-driving accident."

I felt my breath stop. My throat tightened. I wanted to disappear.

"I'm so sorry," I finally managed to say.

"That's okay," he said.

There was another long silence then, but this one didn't feel so great. My heart was pumping double time. I wanted somehow to make this moment okay.

"I told you sooner or later you'd want me to shut up." My voice sounded small and weak now.

But Eric stopped walking and turned toward me. I stopped, too. His eyes were soft and almost smiling, and he took my mittened hand in his.

"Seriously, Sam, it's okay," he said. "I wanted to tell you. I think that's why I reacted so strongly to you and your . . . stepmom."

"Yeah, I guess that seems pretty silly, when you think about . . . I'm sorry."

"No, I didn't say that to make you feel bad. Please." Eric held my arm, and I could feel his eyes without looking at him. "And if I wanted to, I could've easily lied. But

I wanted to tell you, because . . . I don't know. I felt like you'd get it."

"I do. I think," I said.

Then we came to a dense clump of trees. Eric ducked his head under a branch and went in, with me right behind. The trees were so tightly woven overhead that there was barely any snow on the ground in here. Just a bed of pine needles that crackled and crunched under our feet. Eric stopped and looked up.

"This is my favorite spot. There's a quiet out here that I can't find anywhere else."

He put his hands on my shoulders and led me into the center of the patch. Then he came around and faced me again, this time lifting his head up to the sky, his eyes closed. I did the same. He was right. There was an incredible hush all around us, like the whole world stopped within these trees. It felt like I could hear each snowflake landing and gently melting. Like I could hear to the other end of the world, but was protected from it all in this peaceful cocoon.

Eric took in a deep breath. And then I pictured him standing there in front of me, his eyes closed, too. And now I could hear my heart pounding, pounding.

Levy! What was that about?

I wondered if Eric could hear it, too. I opened my eyes. He was still standing there, only now he was looking right at me, his eyes the most spectacular, earthy green. Completely open and so honest that I had to look away into the trees.

"Wow," I whispered. "Do you come here a lot?"

Ugh, Levy! Really smooth. But at least I hadn't said, "What's your sign?"

"As often as I can," he said.

"By yourself?"

"Well, Fozzie."

"Have you ever slept out here?"

"Yeah, once or twice."

"By yourself?"

"Sure."

He started laughing softly.

"Sam?" he said.

"Yeah?" I looked back over at him. He was smiling.

"Never mind," he said. "You okay to go a little farther?"

"I think so."

We came out of the trees and followed a path through a narrow opening between two big boulders. The land unfolded in front of us in glittering white hills.

It was hard to tell where the mountains ended and the sky began. We kept on walking, the snow swirling all around us.

"Look at that!" Eric whispered as we came near another bunch of trees, putting his arm out to stop me. There was a deer hiding behind one of the pine trunks, every muscle in her body still except for her tail flicking wildly. She was the most beautiful shade of chestnut, with long, sculpted legs. I felt like I could see every muscle in her body even as she stood there. Then her head moved sharply, like she heard something in the wind, and she galloped off.

We continued on. We walked for miles, I'm sure of it. And I could've kept on going miles more. Eric stopped when we got to a ledge overlooking a small valley.

"Come here. Get a good look," he said. I stepped forward slowly.

The view was spectacular. There was a small village below us, rooftops covered in a silky-smooth white, and chimneys with puffs of blue-gray smoke drifting up into the sky. Trees bent together under the weight of the newly fallen snow. It was coming down really fast now, melting on my cheeks, my nose, my eyes.

"Oh, I would love to live there," I sighed.

"Yeah, that would be fun, huh?" said Eric. And then I felt his hand gently rest on the small of my back. It was that place just below my ribs where my mom used to rub me as I fell asleep at night. She had the gentlest hands, the smoothest touch. If I was crying or scared or I just couldn't fall asleep, it was always the spot that soothed me. Nobody since then had ever touched me there. Until this moment. And now, even through my thermals, my sweater, my jacket, I could feel my spine tingling.

"Well, I guess maybe we should head back. It *is* coming down pretty thick," Eric said.

It was true. It looked like one of those snow globes that Ashley was talking about, and it was getting hard to see. Still, I didn't want to turn around. I didn't want our afternoon to end. But, of course, I said, "Okay."

Eric called out Fozzie's name. I had forgotten all about him. There was a rustling in a small line of trees ahead of us and then Fozzie leaped out, bobbing over mounds of snow, his coat white and sparkly.

"Good boy," said Eric, rubbing him down. He fished into his pocket and pulled out a piece of bacon for him. Fozzie jumped up and down, licking his lips. "Home, boy! We're going home!"

Without missing a beat, Fozzie started back in the direction of the inn.

"He knows the way," said Eric.

We walked back in silence. The wind had picked up now and was blowing everything sideways. Fozzie had his head to the ground, and I could only see his tail at some points. The whole left side of my face was soon wet and frozen. My left eye was caked in snow and I could feel my eyelashes frozen together. But I didn't care. I loved every minute of it. I loved the knowledge that Eric and Fozzie and I were walking through this storm *together.* It felt like we were explorers, like Lewis and Clark or maybe Ernest Shackleton, and we were marching toward new lands and new heights.

"There's gold up in them thar hills!" I said into the wind at one point. I know, dork. I had heard it in one of those films they make you watch in history class. It made Phoebe laugh whenever I said it.

I didn't count on Eric hearing me, to be honest. But then he called back, "By Jove, we'll find it. Even if we have to die tryin'!" and then we both laughed, even though that meant swallowing a bunch of wet snow.

By the time we got back to the inn, the sky was a deep plum color and there were thick piles of snow against the back door, draped over the lamps, the porch, the eaves.

"Where were you?" Martha cried, taking Eric's face in her hands. "We were so worried about you! Come here! Come here!" She helped us peel off our jackets and we went into a small pantry, where we could leave our drenched boots and scarves, hats, and mittens. Then Martha gave us fluffy blue towels to help us dry off. Luis toweled off Fozzie, pulling clumps of ice out of his paws.

"Your father called from Burlington. He said he was going to stay put until the storm died down a little," Martha told Eric. Then she turned to me. "And your father called to say they were at the chalet eating French fries, waiting for the plows to come through. I didn't tell either of them that I thought you got buried by an avalanche. Look at you! You must be freezing! Can I make you something to eat? I bet you're starving. What if we pull out some of these new groceries and make a picnic here in the kitchen?"

"Sounds good," said Eric. "We'll help."

I went upstairs and changed into another pair of jeans and my warmest sweater. Then the four of us pulled out fresh mozzarella and roasted peppers, green olives, avocados, and crisp spinach. Martha sliced up a long baguette that was still steaming from the oven. Luis opened a bottle of red wine. "Ssh, don't tell your papa, Eric," he said smiling.

We pulled up stools in front of the big island in the middle of the room and just ate and drank and talked and laughed. This time I was careful to take small sips of the wine. Martha and Luis told us about meeting in Florence. Martha had been traveling with her girlfriends after college. Her parents were very nervous about her going that far away, and she was only supposed to be there for a month, but instead she stayed ten years. We heard about their kids, their grandkids, the house they had in Scudderville, where there was a squirrel living in their roof and a shed where Luis was trying to make a rocking chair.

"He's been working on that damn chair for three years now," said Martha. "At this point it should rock itself."

"I'm almost done," he said, nudging her in the side.

"I hope I see it before I die," she said, grinning. Her teeth were stained purple from the wine.

For the rest of the afternoon, Eric and I sat in front of the fire. Eric brought down a game of Scrabble and we played on the coffee table. I got thirty-four points for the word *apex* but he still beat me with a triple word score on *juggle*. Then we just sat and stared at the fire some more. Fozzie was snoring and making little *yip yip* sounds in his sleep. I wondered what he was dreaming about.

I started dozing, too, until Martha came through the door.

"For you, my dear!" she sang, handing me the house phone.

"Hello?"

"Hey, chicken," said Dad. "We just got the okay. Plows are almost through. We'll be there in about a half hour."

"Okay," I said, and clicked off.

I looked at Eric.

"What is it?"

"The roads are clear. They're coming home." I put a smile on my face, but it felt pasted on. All I could think about was how much I didn't want this to end. I just wanted to hold on to the glow of the fire, the sound of Martha and Luis chatting in the kitchen, the smell of garlic and butter floating under the door, and Eric in the chair next to me.

Agh, Levy! Didn't you learn anything from that whole Drew experience? Guys are either unavailable emotionally or total horndogs.

But that didn't seem really fair to Eric. I mean, he had started out kind of bossy, but that all made sense now. And now that we had spent some time together, I thought he was pretty funny, especially when he pretended he was Fozzie and said things like, "I'm the mayor of this town and I declare that we should all eat yellow snow and then take naps for the rest of the day!"

And he had a great laugh and he also said (as Eric) that he liked how I was full of stories and he thought my turtle hat was fantastic. And his fingers were long and skinny and stained with ink. . . .

"Hey! Will you show me some of your drawings?" I asked, sitting up straight now.

Eric shook his head. "Nah, that's boring. Don't you want to just relax before the others get back?"

"No. I really want to see them. Come on, please?" It felt urgent now. Like a need, somehow.

"If you insist." Eric smiled.

He went up the back stairs behind Phil's office and brought down a large black sketchbook. It was frayed at the edges and held together by a big rubber band with pages slipping out of all sides.

"I can't believe you want to see this stuff," he mumbled. "Please promise me you'll stop me before I bore you to tears."

"Promise," I said.

We settled down on the rug, and he opened up the worn cover. The drawings were breathtaking. They were of snow-covered mountains — but not like, here are some trees, here's some snow. Each branch, each pine needle was so delicate and exact. I could smell the cold air, the wet bark. Then there was one of Fozzie as he lay on his beanbag bed, every hair placed just so. A series of sunsets behind a line of trees and even though they were all in charcoal, I could see the colors — the orange melting into pink into lilac into nothing. He turned the page.

"Ah, you don't have to see that one."

"What?" I said, tugging at his sleeve.

"Nothing," he said, pulling back more pages. I tugged again.

"Come on."

He stopped, took a breath.

"Okay, but just . . . yeah, whatever." I saw little splotches of color in his cheeks, right next to his ears. Why was he blushing?

He opened the pad again. The page was full of all different shades of light and dark. It was hard to adjust my eyes at first, but then I saw the lines come together, the faces find their space, the shadows take shape, inhabiting the page. And when I did, I saw . . .

"That's . . . that's . . ." He had drawn all of us singing that night at karaoke. When he was sitting in the back, watching. There was Liz in the front, Heidi and Dina behind her, and me in the back. It was so detailed, so intricate. The light was exactly like it had felt up there in front of the microphone. I could see Liz's hips swaying, her blond locks shaking, her cheeks full and bright. There was the fire blazing and the two lamps and the moose head over the mantel. Heidi and Dina had their mouths open and their hands on their hips. He had even drawn the windows to the left, and the dark of the night beyond. Everything was there. I felt like I could hear the music thumping, feel the beat pulsing, touch the energy of the room. He had completely captured the moment.

And there was me — my face tipped up to the ceiling, my eyes closed, my lips in a circle as if I was singing "ooooh." I stared at the picture.

"The perspective's a little off," he said quietly. "It was dark."

And now I felt myself flushing, too. "Did I really look like that?" I whispered. It looked like there was light bouncing off my skin. My hair shimmered down my shoulders and through the cracks of my eyes there was the faintest glimmer. I looked . . . beautiful.

"Yeah," he said. "You did to me."

"Wow," I said. "I mean, thanks." And then we sat there, looking at that night. It was only a few days ago, but things were so different now. I had thought he was such a weirdo and a creep sitting back there with the flickering candle in the dark. And he must've thought — Wow. What *had* he thought? I wanted to ask him. Actually, I wanted to ask him what he was thinking right now, too.

"Sam?" he whispered.

"Yeah?" I croaked.

"I just wondered if you still thought I was kind of a nosy jerk," he said, facing the fire.

I almost laughed. It was so much the opposite of

what I was thinking. But I didn't want him to think that I was laughing at him.

"Not at all," I said. "And do you still think I'm a rude girl who doesn't know when to keep her mouth shut?"

I stayed looking at the fire too, but I could see Eric smile out of the corner of my eye.

"I never did," he said.

A blast of cold air came through the front door.

"Whew! What a day!"

"Oh, there's still a fire, good!"

"Please, someone give me something — anything — to eat besides a French fry!"

The guests started spilling into the lobby, shedding their coats and standing in front of the fire. They seemed to be totally oblivious to the fact that we were sitting there. I saw Fozzie look up wearily and then trot off to find some other, more secluded spot for sleeping.

"Hey, kiddo! Thought we'd never see you again. How's my girl?" Dad pulled me up and took my face in his hands.

"Good. Great."

"You feeling better?" asked Kathy.

"Yeah, much." This time, I really didn't mean to be

rude, but I wanted to see if Eric was still in the chair next to me, getting gobbled up by everybody crowding in and talking about the storm. He must've gone into the kitchen to help Martha and Luis with dinner, though.

"Soup's on!" I heard Martha holler, and everyone started shuffling toward the dining room.

I didn't see Eric again for the rest of the night. Well okay, except for when I lay in bed later and closed my eyes. I saw those long, stained fingers and that crooked nose and him saying softly, "I never did."

And then I giggled a little as I whispered out into the night, "What did *that* mean?"

Chapter 18

“What do you say, kid? Last day to hit the slopes. You coming?” asked Dad, putting down his coffee cup.

Our last day! I couldn’t believe it. Dad looked at me expectantly. What I really felt like doing was hanging out here with Eric and Fozzie. But I couldn’t say that. And where was Eric, anyway? My window looked out on the back and I had happened to see him early that morning taking off in his truck. He still hadn’t come back, as far as I knew. It’s not like we had planned to see each other today, anyway. But I felt excited and nervous, but mostly excited to see him again. Okay, and nervous. And confused.

“What do you think? Should we try Seneca Mountain today?”

"I'm in!" said Jeremy. I think he was really sore from his snowboarding expedition, but I knew he would never admit it.

"Me too!" said Kathy.

Dad turned to me. What could I say? That I might sorta maybe run into a guy that I *had* thought was the biggest jerk on earth and now I was too scared to even say his name?

"Yeah, okay."

Seneca Mountain was actually a series of slopes, folding on top of one another, each peak reaching higher into the sky. We decided we would all try cross-country for the morning. Dad said it would be easy for me and Jeremy to learn, which was fine with me. Just looking at the downhill trails made me a little uneasy, and I noticed Jeremy was walking kind of funny, like there were balloons stuck between his legs or something, but I resisted the urge to make fun of him.

We got our skis and then made our way out to the bottom of the main slope to wait for the chairlift. This place was definitely off the beaten track — it wasn't nearly as crowded as Sugar Peak. Just open sky and mountains cascading down on every side. It was glorious. I really wanted to be sharing it with Dad, but somehow he wound up talking to Jeremy in the back of the line and before I knew it, Kathy and I were sliding into a chair and being whisked up and away.

"Ah. Sure is magnificent up here," she said, shielding her eyes with her gloved hand.

"Yeah," I said. I wasn't sure how long the lift was, but I wondered if we could talk about the scenery the whole time. It hit me then that the two of us had barely spoken the whole week.

She was tapping her fingers quickly on her legs. I guess we were both at a loss for words. "Have you had fun up here?" she asked finally.

"Yeah, yeah."

"I am just so impressed with how fast you and Jeremy picked this stuff up. I mean, I'm still terrified of downhill."

"Oh, you know." I honestly didn't mean to be incommunicative. I was just thinking about a million other things right then.

"Did you used to —" Kathy began. And then, halfway through her sentence, the car lurched forward and stopped.

"What was that?" I gasped.

"I'm not sure," she said. She put a smile on her face but I could see there was panic in her eyes. We were somewhere past the tops of the trees, dangling about a gazillion feet over the ground. Okay, maybe that was an exaggeration, but we were a long way up.

"Attention skiers! Attention skiers!" There was someone on a megaphone at the bottom of the slope. "We are experiencing some difficulty with the chairlift. Please remain in your seats with your hands on the bar and we will fix this as soon as possible!"

"What does that mean? Difficulty?" I stammered.

"I'm not quite sure," said Kathy slowly.

I like to think of myself as a fairly level-headed person. I don't burst into tears that often, and I know what to do in case of a fire. I'll always volunteer to be in the exit row on a plane, and I know how to treat a nosebleed. But I guess I am not the best companion during a real crisis. It's this head of mine. It just keeps on spinning. How were they going to get us out of there? Would they take us out by air lift or would we have to swing from a rope like Tarzan or *what*? I didn't know how to climb down a rope. I mean, we did that in gym class once but I never got the hang of it and then our teacher,

Mr. Stern, was sick the next day so we just watched movies on schoolyard safety. Oh, I hoped they didn't give us a rope. Or maybe a giant net? Could they do that? Did we sign waivers or something?

And then my mouth started flapping.

"I mean, does this happen a lot? Do they know what they're doing? What if it doesn't get unstuck? Do they have a plan of some sort?"

I knew Kathy didn't have any of these answers, but I couldn't help myself. And now we were slowly rocking back and forth, somewhere in midair.

"Hey, Sam! Kathy! You all right?"

Dad's voice came from somewhere behind us. I forgot that we were *all* caught up here, hanging by that tiny wire.

"Yeah!" we called back in unison, and then we both laughed a little. It actually felt good to laugh.

"Don't worry! The guy behind us says this happens a lot! It'll get cleared up soon!"

I closed my eyes and tried to focus my breath. *In, 2, 3. Out, 2, 3. In, 2, 3. Out, 2, 3.*

Then I felt Kathy touch my knee. I opened my eyes.

"It's gonna be okay, Sam," she said.

"Yeah, I know," I said.

"I mean . . . with us." She looked me right in the eye now. Her gaze was steady and calm.

"Yeah," I said. I didn't know what else to say.

"I mean, we both have a lot to learn about each other. I'm scared, too, you know. I never expected — did you ever hear how your dad and I met?"

"No."

I had never even asked. I had been too busy being mad. That first phone call when he told me he'd started seeing someone and he thought — he hoped — I would like her. I was sitting on the floor of my bedroom, and I remember hanging up on him so I could cry.

"Do you want to know?" she asked gently, watching my face, which I know was lost in thought.

"Yes. Yes," I said. And I meant it.

"Well, let me first say this. I wasn't supposed to fall in love with someone fourteen years older than me — with two kids and a mortgage and a tan sedan. No offense, but that's just not how I had imagined it." She laughed. She was really pretty, especially when she laughed. And then she stopped herself. "Are you sure it's okay that I'm telling you this?" she asked.

I nodded again. "Please," I said.

"Okay, well, the first thing that happened was he

took my parking spot outside the travel agency. I always parked in the same spot, right on the corner of Degraw and Lafayette. And one day, I was running late to work, as usual, and your father cut me off. Oooh, I was so mad! I rolled down my window and I was screaming all sorts of names at him. It was not pretty."

She giggled and rolled her dark eyes. I thought of the way I had snapped at Eric that first night outside on the steps.

"And your father, gentle soul that he is, pulled out after me, followed me around the corner and all the way down the hill, where I finally found a parking spot. I didn't notice that he was behind me, of course, until I got out of the car and there he was. I was in such a rush, I remember, I slammed my bag in the car door. I was cursing like a sailor. And then when I saw him standing there, wow, I really laid into him. 'I park there every day!' and 'Don't you have any common courtesy?' And I remember I ended it by saying, 'And now it looks like you're following me!' And then, he waited for me to finish, with those beautiful, patient eyes, and he looked at me and said, 'You are absolutely right. I am following you. Because you were right, and I was wrong. And I'd like the chance to make it up to you.'"

"Wow," I said. "That's pretty — wow." The thought of my dad being Mr. Romance was kind of funny. But sweet.

"Yeah." She grinned. "And still I wasn't having it. He handed me a slip of paper, and I took it and walked off in such a huff. Ha! But later that day, I remember sitting at my desk with that slip of paper he had given me. Just his name and number. And then underneath he had written, 'I've never tried this before.' And I thought, 'What just happened to me?' There was something so honest, so unafraid about that note and those eyes. I felt sick, and excited, and confused, and like my heart was up in my ears."

Sick, and excited, and confused. It was all sounding so familiar.

"Okay, I'm talking too much, but one more thing. Sam, I was never good at dating. I mean, look. It took me thirty-eight years to find your dad. And I was with some real duds before him, believe me. And then when I did find him, I was so scared! There is *nothing* scarier than having real feelings for someone. I mean, it can swoop in and lift you off your feet and turn you upside down. Sometimes it leaves you breathless and hopeful, and sometimes it can tear you in two. But you know what? It is always, always worth it. It feels a lot like this, actually. Way up high, almost touching the clouds, suspended. Not knowing what's going to happen next." She sighed. "I don't know. Does that make sense at all?"

"Oh, yes," I said. It made so much sense I wanted to press her words into my skin. I looked out around us at the mountains, the trees, our feet swaying out in front of us. It was all so unpredictable. I didn't know whether I wanted to laugh or cry or howl into the breeze. And then I thought of Eric. I could never have predicted that. That? This? Well, whatever it was. But now I knew it was *something.*

I had always imagined that liking someone was about something just out of reach. An ache, a longing, like when I had pined for Leo. But maybe the ones who were worth it were the ones who didn't make you try so hard. They liked you for who you were. And they didn't really know any more than you. Nobody truly had the answers. It was all about taking the leap, together.

I watched as Kathy leaned her face up into the sun. Her skin looked like melting honey, each of her eye-lashes illuminated. She didn't know what she was doing either. I closed my eyes and tilted my head up, too. And

I knew we looked nothing alike, nobody would ever mistake us for mother and daughter, but sitting up there, both of our faces raised to the sun, maybe we could just be friends.

A little while later, I felt another jolt. The chairs started swinging forward and back again.

"Whoa!" Kathy said, grabbing the crossbar so tight her knuckles turned bright white. I did the same. And then, with a low creak and groan from below, we slowly started inching up the mountain. I heard a pitter-patter sound climbing up behind us. Was that rain? Wasn't it too cold for that?

"Look! Look!" said Kathy, pointing down to the bottom of the lift. It wasn't rain at all. It was a small gathering of people down below, in all different-colored hats and jackets. And they were waving and clapping for us. We were on our way!

The rest of the day, Dad and Kathy took us through densely wooded trails, each one more beautiful than the next. Cross-country was hard, but in a new, invigorating way. I felt my legs, my arms, my lungs all pumping, pulling, working together. By the time we got done for the day, I was exhausted, and dying to get back to the inn.

Eric was behind the bar in the living room, pouring

drinks for happy hour. I didn't even take off my jacket. I walked right up to the counter while he had his back turned.

"Double shot of amaretto and orange juice, and a splash of rye."

"Sorry?" He spun around and broke into a big smile. A big, crooked smile.

"Do you think I could talk to you for a minute?" I asked quietly now. "I need to tell you something."

"Yeah," he said. "But first, I have something that I forgot to show you. Wait right there." And he disappeared into the kitchen.

When he came back out, he had on his jacket, too.

"Come on." He led me out through the sliding door. We pushed out into the night. The snow was up to our knees in the field, and there were still a few feathery flakes slipping down out of the sky. The moon looked like a creamy shell, set in the deep blue-black of the night, scattering bright beams down onto the gleaming snow.

Then, without a word, Eric took my mittened hand in his. I felt a tremor through my arm. He clicked on the flashlight, and we headed out across the field. I didn't ask him where we were going or what we were doing. It didn't matter. I knew that even if he brought me out here to see a pinecone I would be just glad to be out here — with him. We walked down the backyard and over the little hill. Then across the creek, still trickling now through islands of snow and ice. Up into the Gallaghers' farm. Past the house. We came to the quiet tangle of trees at the bottom of their land, and Eric led me in.

The pine needles felt slippery and thin. Through a tiny opening in the branches above I could see the moonlight and just a few stray flakes of snow sailing to earth. And there was that hush in here. A calm that was now somehow electric.

Eric stopped and turned toward me, taking both my hands in his.

"So I know I showed you this place before, but there was something I forgot to do when we were here and I just wanted to, before, well . . . if it's okay . . ."

I watched his face carefully. I didn't dare move a muscle. And then, in that moment, as he leaned in, the whole world got swallowed up by the stillness of those trees. His lips dissolved into mine, and I felt every inch of my body light up, all of me glowing a vibrant, pure white. I closed my eyes and melted into the greatest kiss in the history of the world.

We stayed like that for I don't know how long. I lost

all sense of time and space. But I do know that at some point his lips started quivering. And then he pulled away, laughing softly.

"What?" I said, afraid.

Levy! What did you do?

Had I slobbered all over him? Did I eat a filling?

"No, nothing! I'm just so happy," he said.

I sighed with relief. He touched his forehead to mine, our noses pressed together.

"Now, sorry. What did you want to tell me?" he whispered.

"Just . . . this."

I pulled his face toward mine. And this time *I* was kissing *him,* and I was sure of myself. My lips, my teeth, my tongue. They were right where they should be. We stayed like that for a long time. For a really long time, and yet it all went by so fast. And then, just as I began to pull away, I felt it. At first I couldn't tell what it was. I felt an itch, like someone was tickling me, just under my nose. And then a coldness, melting, and I knew. It was a single snowflake drifting down and landing just where our lips met, nesting there, between us. My heart lifted and fluttered open. I had found it. The snowflake I was supposed to kiss.

"Hey, Eric?"

"Yeah."

"I just have to say, I don't really know what I'm doing." Yeah, it wasn't exactly original. But it was a great line.

And I didn't know if I meant physically, or mentally, or what. I just knew I needed to say it.

Eric smiled.

"I don't either," he said.

And then we kissed some more. Deep, long, kisses. And held each other, standing up, in the world's quietest place.

"Hey, listen," he whispered at one point. He took my hand and put it on his chest. I could feel his heart beating through his jacket and it matched mine — fast and strong.

"It's goin' nuts, huh?" he said.

I wanted to say *Wait! Are you for real?* Or *You're here! You're here!* Or *What does this mean?* Or *Help! I'm supposed to leave tomorrow!* But I kept my lips together.

Just let it be, Levy.

We were both there in that unknowing. In that possibility.

And then he took my hand and we silently walked back to the inn.

Chapter 19

It was a good thing our flight wasn't until the early afternoon, because when Dad's phone call woke me up, I was nowhere near ready. As a matter of fact, I was still in my clothes from the night before. Eric and I had stayed up until at least three in the morning talking in front of that fire. I looked around the room. The rest of my clothes were strewn all over. Sweaters, jeans, socks drooping over the chair.

"Meet you downstairs in ten?" said Dad.

"Yup," I said, and then started throwing things in my bag while I brushed my teeth.

Fozzie was the first one to greet me at the bottom of the stairs.

"He's been waiting for you all morning," said Eric,

coming up behind him. His eyes looked particularly big and green and spectacular this morning.

"Hey, Fozzie. I'm gonna miss you," I managed. I was already feeling hollow just thinking about leaving him.

Dad, Kathy, and Jeremy were having breakfast in our usual spot.

"Can I go for one last walk before we pack up?" I asked.

Kathy looked up and smiled. Did she know about me and Eric . . . ?

"Sure," said Dad.

Eric and I followed Fozzie out into the backyard. He bounded across the field, with us walking slowly behind. Eric took my mitten in his hand.

"So," he said.

"So, yeah," I said back.

We walked for a while not saying anything. Amazingly, he was the one who spoke first. "What do you think?" His voice was low.

"I don't know. I mean, I wasn't supposed to meet somebody like you," I said.

"You mean devastatingly handsome, fascinating, and a lover of fine cheeses?" He squeezed my hand and gave me a mischievous grin.

I punched him on the arm lightly. "I mean, I was just supposed to go away with my dad and Kathy and Jeremy. Maybe learn how to ski. But this feels . . ." I didn't know how to finish the sentence. Maybe I was making this into more than what it was. I really hoped not.

"Yeah, it feels like we might've just started something big, you know? I mean . . . I hope. Maybe," he said.

And now my stomach was doing cartwheels and my heart was beating so loud I could feel it in my toes.

Levy, hold it together. But I was dying to say something.

"Me too! I mean, yes. I mean, I think so, too."

"Yeah," he said. I could feel the smiles on both of our faces.

We walked some more. Just to the edge of the Gallaghers' plot though. My dad had given me strict instructions that we had to be in the car in twenty-five minutes. He's crazy about getting to airports two years before the flight.

"Guess we gotta turn around," said Eric.

"Yup."

He kissed my mittened hand.

"Hey, I'm gonna call you tonight. To make sure you get home okay. Is that all right?" he asked.

"I'd like that."

"And maybe while you're up in the air, just so I can hear your voice mail."

I giggled. "Sounds good to me."

"And maybe right now, just to make sure I've got your number."

I reached into my pocket to get my phone. I hadn't touched it in days. I only remembered it because it fell out of my sweatshirt when I had gone to throw it in my suitcase. I looked at it now. Seven more missed calls. What? I opened it up. They were all from Phoebe.

"What is it?" asked Eric.

"Oh, my friend Phoebe. The one I told you about." I had told him about Phoebe, but just briefly. I didn't want to tell him just the bad parts. I knew there was a lot more to our friendship than just the past few days. At least, I thought so.

"You think you should call her?" he said.

"I will," I said. "But for now, I want to be right here."

When we got back to the inn, Dad was already packing up the rental car. Eric went inside to get Fozzie some food. He said he'd be back out in just a few minutes. I went in to grab a muffin and some coffee. I had decided once I got home that I was going to tell my mom to start making an extra cup for me in the morning. I was an adult, after all. And besides, if it stunted my growth, that was fine. I was already almost six feet tall.

Eric came back into the dining room and joined me by a window.

"Okay! All set!" sang Dad, coming in behind him. Kathy quickly ran in, too. She winked at me.

"Actually," said Kathy, "I think the trunk isn't closing all the way. Can you give me a hand please, Judd?" She grabbed Dad's arm and pulled him toward the front door.

"She's really pretty cool," said Eric.

"Yeah, she's okay. It's a good thing someone butt his nose in and told me to give her a chance," I said, smiling.

He pulled out a piece of paper from his coat pocket.

"Well, I just wanted to give you this. It's nothing big. I'm not much for good-byes, you know? So, how about I just say, I'll talk to you tonight, and then I'll see you soon, and we'll . . . um . . . take it from there."

"Yeah, sounds good."

"I mean, once the busy season slows down a little, maybe I could take a drive down to New York with Fozzie. Like in March or April?"

"I'd like that a lot."

"Yeah." He swallowed.

"I'd *really* like that a lot." I didn't think I could say much more. And then, he just held me again with those arms. Those arms that had picked me up and led me down the mountain and into the most beautiful place I had ever been. And I breathed him in, the smell of his warm neck, like fir trees and cedar wood. I tried to take it all in. To hold it deep inside.

In the car, I waited until we were up the hill and past the main square of town. "Good-bye" I whispered to the snow-covered steeples and Canfield Corners. The road extended out in front of us like a dark ribbon between the mounds of fresh snow, the trees bending together to whisper among their branches. Dad was whistling and he had one hand on Kathy's knee, keeping time to his tune. It slipped from "Paperback Writer" to "Eleanor Rigby" this time. Jeremy was leaning back and staring out at the mountains again. A low cloud of bluish-gray hung above the peaks, heavy with another snow about to fall.

I turned toward my window and slowly pulled out

the piece of paper, then unfolded it delicately, spreading it out on my lap. It was a charcoal drawing of a girl, her head upturned, her eyes closed, her lips making a small circle. Her hair fell down long and straight across her shoulders. Her arms were outstretched and above her fell speckled bits of snow caught in midair.

It was me. I knew it was. But until this trip, I had never seen myself this way before. So relaxed, so care-free, so beautiful.

I turned the picture over.

Dear Sam,

I'm not sure what to say. As you said, "I'm not good at this." But I just wanted to say, thank you for everything. For screaming at me outside. For sipping coffee by the fire. For walking to the Gallaghers' farm with me and for sharing my favorite place in the world. For falling down and for picking me up. But most of all, thank you for teaching me how to kiss snowflakes. I hope we can do that again soon.

Love, Eric

I folded the paper back up and brought it to my lips.

That was one snowflake I hoped would never melt.

Craving more winter romance?

Be sure to check out MISTLETOE: FOUR HOLIDAY STORIES, featuring Hailey Abbott, Melissa de la Cruz, Aimee Friedman, and Nina Malkin!

Below, take a sneak peek at Aimee Friedman's story, "Working in a Winter Wonderland."

As Maxine wandered the crowded aisles of the holiday market, her eyes flicking over displays of beaded necklaces, velour gloves, and fat, scented candles, she wondered if a winter-break job might be the best solution to her money woes. After all, she reasoned, her home life was driving her nuts, and her social life would be laughable until New Year's. If only she had the slightest idea where to find work. She cast a glance at a nearby stall selling hideous winter hats, as if a HELP WANTED sign might be hanging there.

A sudden, near-arctic wind tore through the market, rattling a display of glass bowls. "Damn, it's *cold*!" someone cried in a Southern accent — a tourist, Maxine guessed, who'd been under the mistaken impression that New York City would be balmy on December 17. Shivering, Maxine hurried over to the hat stand, cursing herself for leaving her cloche hat somewhere in her messy bedroom. *Whatever*, she decided as she selected a fuzzy leopard-print number with earflaps. *I'd rather look like a first-class freak than die of hypothermia.* She was adjusting the hat on her head when she heard a familiar male voice behind her.

"Madeline? Madeline Silverman?"

Oh, God. Can it be —

Turning very slowly, Maxine found herself staring

into the almond-shaped, bright hazel eyes of Heath Barton.

Yes, Heath Barton. His glossy jet-black hair blew across his dark eyebrows and a smile played on his full lips. Maxine noticed that his leather jacket hung open, revealing a black turtleneck and black jeans ripped at the knees. Dazedly, she wondered why he wasn't freezing, until she realized that his own out-of-this-world hotness must have been keeping him nice and toasty. Maxine felt *her* body temperature climbing by the second.

"Madeline," Heath repeated with utter assurance, his square-jawed face now breaking into a wide grin. "From high school. You remember me, right?"

You could say that.

"Oh . . . sure," Maxine said, doing her best imitation of breeziness. She cocked her head to one side, studying him. "Heath . . . Barton, is it?" As he nodded, eyes glinting, she added, "And it's not Madeline, by the way. I'm Maxine. Maxine Silver."

Not that she necessarily expected Heath Barton to remember her name. Back in high school, he'd been the ringleader of the rich-boy slackers and always had some pouty groupie — Maxine had nicknamed them

"Heathies" — on his arm. Ensconced in her artsy circle of friends, Maxine had outwardly mocked Heath and his ilk, but went all jelly-kneed at the sight of him. And there'd been certain moments that Maxine had caught Heath shooting her inquisitive glances that had clearly meant *Hmm . . . maybe sometime.* Maxine had been counting on New Year's, but maybe the time was, well, right now.

Or could have been now, had she not been wearing a leopard-print hat with earflaps.

Just as Maxine's hands were reaching up to remove the unfortunate accessory, Heath stepped forward, eliminating the space between them. "Maxine — that's right," he said, laughing softly. "My bad. I was close though, huh?"

He was certainly getting close. Maxine barely had time to notice that Heath smelled like wood smoke and cider and spice — and that he'd somehow become even hotter since high school — before he plucked the ridiculous hat off her head, his fingers brushing her sideswept bangs. As he set the hat down on the counter behind them, Maxine frantically tried to mash her post-hat hair back into some semblance of place.

"Don't do that." Heath chuckled, turning back to her. "You're ruining the cuteness effect."

Oh, damn. Maxine wasn't a big blusher, but now she felt an unavoidable warmth stealing up her neck.

"So catch me up, Maxine Silver," Heath drawled, resting one elbow on the counter as his eyes held hers. "College adventures, crimes, scandals, holiday plans?"

Maxine shrugged. "You know, the usual, I guess," she replied, hoping the conversation would steer its way back to the subject of her supposed cuteness.

"I'm *stoked* to be out of New Haven," Heath confessed with a world-weary sigh, running a hand through his floppy hair. "There's nothing like winter in the city — chilling with my boys, helping out my dad at his store —" Heath paused meaningfully, and raised an eyebrow at Maxine. "Oh — I'm not sure if you know who my dad — I mean —" He ducked his head.

Maxine nodded. "I know," she whispered. *Everyone* knew who Heath's father was: Cecil Barton III, owner of Barton's, the sumptuous jewel box of a department store on Fifth Avenue. Maxine remembered the buzz Mr. Barton, in his bow tie and bowler hat, had created at their graduation alongside Heath's mother, who was an equally famous — and stunning — Japanese former supermodel.

"I'm actually here for my dad today," Heath was saying, as if he'd read her mind. "Doing market research —

to check out the competition and all." With a slight air of distaste, he gestured to the packed stalls around them. "Technically I'm supposed to be on my lunch break but we're so swamped at the store that I've got to mix business with pleasure." Maxine was forcing herself not to fixate on the word *pleasure* coming out of Heath's mouth when he rolled his long-lashed eyes and went on. "It's madness over there — one of the salesgirls quit this morning so the manager wasn't giving me a moment's rest. I was all like, 'Mr. Perry, can I at least get a ciggie break?' and he was like —"

"Wait." The word had escaped Maxine's lips almost without her realizing it. *Swamped at the store. Salesgirl quit*. She felt inspiration flooding through her body, making her skin prickle and her breath catch. She found she couldn't move. "There's — there's an opening at Barton's?" she asked. Furiously, her mind fought to process this incredible piece of information. An opening, just when she most needed a job? An opening at the very place where *Heath Barton himself was working*?

"Uh-huh," Heath said distractedly, reaching into his jacket pocket and pulling out a sleek BlackBerry. Then he lifted his head and met Maxine's gaze, which she knew must have been wild-eyed and borderline manic. She tried to compose her features into a mask of glamorous sophistication, but then Heath's own eyes widened, and his lips slowly parted. "Maxine, are *you* interested?" he murmured, and then he tilted his head to one side, clearly sizing her up — though for what, Maxine wasn't sure. Then Heath spoke again, sending all the blood rushing to her face.

"You'd be perfect," was what Heath Barton said. "Perfect for the position."

The flattery roared in Maxine's ears, half-drowning out the rest of what Heath was saying — something about how she should go see Mr. Perry now if she was seriously interested, because those types of positions were usually snatched up right away.

"I can totally stop by Barton's now," Maxine exclaimed, suddenly grateful that her schedule was so empty. "Want to walk back with me?" she added casually, as if the thought of an afternoon stroll with Heath wasn't making her belly flip over.

"I'd love to, Maxine," Heath replied, knitting his brows together. "Only I still need to run a couple of errands for my dad. But hey —" He took another step closer, rested a hand on the sleeve of her corduroy jacket, and gave her arm a small squeeze. "Do good, okay? If you get the position, maybe I'll see you at the store tomorrow?"

Forget *maybe*. Maxine Silver was going for the gold.

She could still feel the warmth of Heath's hand on her arm seconds later, as she flew down Central Park South, passing the glitzy entrances to The Essex House and The Plaza, unable to stop grinning. A shopgirl at Barton's! Visions of free Lola lip glosses, marked-down Rock & Republic jeans, and, most tantalizing of all, daily doses of Heath Barton, danced in her head. Maybe while she was folding sweaters tomorrow morning, Heath would swing by and suggest they mix business and pleasure *together*. Maxine giggled out loud at the thought, prompting a curious glance from an all-blond family waiting in line for a horse-and-carriage ride. Normally Maxine would have ignored them, but she was so suffused with goodwill that she waved a mittened hand at the pigtailed little girl.

Her scarf streaming behind her like a victory flag, Maxine rounded onto Fifth Avenue, where a giant, sparkling white snowflake hung suspended overhead. Panting and a little sweaty from her impromptu workout, Maxine paused and stared up at the snowflake as if it were her personal good-luck pendant. *Please, please let me get the job,* she prayed silently. Then, tossing her head back, Maxine whirled around and pulled open the heavy double doors of Barton's.

To Do List: Read All the Point Books!

By Aimee Friedman

- ❑ South Beach
  0-439-70678-5
- ❑ French Kiss
  0-439-79281-9
- ❑ Hollywood Hills
  0-439-79282-7

By Abby Sher

- ❑ Kissing Snowflakes
  0-545-00010-6

By Hailey Abbott

- ❑ Summer Boys
  0-439-54020-8
- ❑ Next Summer: A Summer Boys Novel
  0-439-75540-9
- ❑ After Summer: A Summer Boys Novel
  0-439-86367-8
- ❑ Last Summer: A Summer Boys Novel
  0-439-86725-8

By Claudia Gabel

- ❑ In or Out
  0-439-91853-7
- ❑ Loves Me, Loves Me Not: An In or Out Novel
  0-439-91854-5

By Nina Malkin

- ❑ 6X: The Uncensored Confessions
  0-439-72421-X
- ❑ 6X: Loud, Fast, & Out of Control
  0-439-72422-8
- ❑ Orange Is the New Pink
  0-439-89965-6

By Pamela Wells

- ❑ The Heartbreakers
  0-439-02691-1

Point

POINTCKLT

I ♥ Bikinis Series

❑ **I ♥ Bikinis: He's with Me**
By Tamara Summers
0-439-91850-2

❑ **I ♥ Bikinis: Island Summer**
By Jeanine Le Ny
0-439-91851-0

❑ **I ♥ Bikinis: What's Hot**
By Caitlyn Davis
0-439-91852-9

By Erin Haft

❑ **Pool Boys**
0-439-83523-2

By Laura Dower

❑ **Rewind**
0-439-70340-9

By Jade Parker

❑ **To Catch a Pirate**
0-439-02694-6

By Randi Reisfeld and H.B. Gilmour

❑ **Oh Baby!**
0-439-67705-X

By Sabrina James

❑ **Secret Santa**
0-439-02695-4

Story Collections

❑ **Fireworks: Four Summer Stories**
By Niki Burnham, Erin Haft, Sarah Mlynowski, and Lauren Myracle
0-439-90300-9

❑ **21 Proms**
Edited by Daniel Ehrenhaft and David Levithan
0-439-89029-2

❑ **Mistletoe: Four Holiday Stories**
By Hailey Abbott, Melissa de la Cruz, Aimee Friedman, and Nina Malkin
0-439-86368-6